# A FINE PAIR OF SHOES AND OTHER STORIES

## A COLLECTION OF SHORT STORIES

### CLARE FLYNN

CRANBROOK PRESS

*For Roland Flynn – witness to many of these being written and my encouraging audience when they were finished.*

# CONTENTS

# FOREWORD

Two of these stories plunder my own family history. A Fine Pair of Shoes started out with my wish to capture and embroider the bare bones of a family story, based on my paternal great-great-grandparents and their trip to The Great Exhibition of 1851. I gave the story away to readers of my books and then decided, on the strength of the feedback, to write a few more.

The Proposal is based on the tragic death of my own maternal grandfather, killed on the Liverpool docks in 1934 when my mother was six.

My novels have so far all been historical but some of these stories are contemporary. I hope you enjoy them.

I have also included the opening chapters to my new novel, The Chalky Sea which is published later in 2017. It's set on the Sussex coast in World War 2.

# A FINE PAIR OF SHOES

ASHTON IN MAKERFIELD, 1851

*S*he'd only worn them once before. After her wedding day she'd stuffed them with tissue paper, wrapped them in a piece of cotton cloth and put them in a box on top of the cupboard. There had never been any call to wear them since, but now she climbed onto the kitchen stool and brought the box down. Wiping away the dust, Elizabeth opened the box and took out the shoes. Cream satin with a silk bow on the front. So dainty. So delicate. They had been her wedding gift from her mother, who'd put a penny aside whenever she could while Elizabeth was growing up, so she would have something that wasn't homemade like the rest of her trousseau.

As she held the shoes, she recalled her wedding day and the mixture of happiness and fear she'd experienced. John Swift had been little more than a stranger to her then. They had exchanged only a few words: their courtship consisting of quick glances, with Elizabeth dropping her gaze whenever there was a risk he might see her looking at him as he walked past her house on the way to the cotton mill where he worked as a spinner. Until one day, after the mill closed he

1

had approached her, raised his cap and asked if he might walk back from church with her the following Sunday. Only a few months later he asked to see her father and made his marriage proposal.

Elizabeth worked in a different mill from John, carding and spooling cotton. The other girls at work put the fear of God in her about what she might expect from marriage – but John had been the best and most considerate husband she could have wished for.

Now after all the years of the shoes lying in state in their box on the top of the cupboard, at last Elizabeth had an occasion to wear them again. Lady Gerard up at the Hall had regaled the women of the town with tales of her visit to the Great Exhibition in London. Her ladyship described the Crystal Palace, filled with every kind of wonder of man's creation from locomotive engines to all the treasures of the Empire. Elizabeth had hurried home afterwards, filled with awe and excitement but never daring to hope that she too might have the chance to visit this magical place.

'Oh, John, you can't imagine what things her ladyship saw at the Great Exhibition. There's everything you can possibly think of – all under one roof. Lady Gerard says we should all do what we can to visit it. Oh, dearest, wouldn't it be a fine thing to be able to go? If only we could. There is even a stuffed elephant. I would be thrilled to see such a thing.'

She looked up at him, then shook her head, knowing such an idea was out of the question.

John reached across the table and took her hands in his.

'Well then, my darling wife, if that's your wish, we will go and see all these wonders for ourselves. I've quite a fancy myself to see a stuffed elephant.'

She jumped up and down in excitement.

'You mean it? All the way to London?'

'If it's good enough for Lady Gerard then it's good

enough for Elizabeth Swift. As it happens, I was going to suggest going – but I didn't think you would want to travel all that way. The Mechanics Institute is arranging transport for as many as wants to go from Ashton. I'll sign us up tomorrow now I know you've a mind to go. There's a big group going from the mill. It will be a bit of an adventure.'

Elizabeth jumped out of her chair and flung her arms around her husband's neck almost knocking him over in her excitement.

She had never set foot outside Ashton-in-Makerfield before and had never expected to do so. John had travelled into Liverpool to visit his brother and had been to Manchester to look at a new type of spinning wheel, but had never travelled further than the borders of Lancashire. The prospect of a journey to the capital city was almost too much for them both to take in.

The Mechanics Institute had arranged a special train to London for hundreds of millworkers. John and Elizabeth were to stay overnight in a lodging house with a full day to visit the Exhibition, before returning home the following day. Three whole days away from Ashton. Elizabeth would have to leave the children behind. Thinking about that, she almost changed her mind, but the eldest was now sixteen and there was also Elizabeth's mother. They'd manage. There would never be another chance like this one in her life. It would be something to tell her grandchildren.

On the morning of their departure, the pair dressed in their Sunday best. Elizabeth put on the cream satin shoes and twirled around in front of her husband and the children.

'Dearest girl, you're not planning to go all the way to London wearing those shoes are you?' said John.

'I certainly am. They're very special shoes.'

'I can see that, my dear, but don't you think you might be more comfortable in your everyday shoes? The Crystal

Palace is said to cover eighteen acres of land so there'll be a lot of walking about. It will be a long day and could be tiring.'

'Nonsense. I wouldn't dream of it. I'm not going all the way to London to mix and mingle with the high and mighty, wearing a pair of old clodhoppers. What on earth do you take me for?'

John shook his head. 'Those are indeed a dainty pair of shoes, but no one's going to see them under your skirts, my love. Wouldn't you rather be comfortable in these?'

Her expression was of outrage. 'Certainly not! I'm wearing these. They're like wearing a pair of soft leather gloves. It will be like walking on air.'

John held up his wife's sensible walking shoes, offering her one last chance to change her mind, then put them back under the bench when he saw the flash of annoyance in her eye.

'You've no sense of romance, John Swift. I bet you don't even remember these shoes do you?'

'I do indeed, dearest. You look as lovely wearing them today as you did when you married me in them all those years ago.'

He leaned down and kissed the top of her head.

She smiled and pushed him away.

'Get away with you, you big daft fella.'

~

THEY STOOD outside the lodging house. John read the painted sign on the wall of the redbrick building.

'This is it. One and threepence a night. Bedstead, woollen mattress, sheets, blankets, coverlets, soap and towels included. Facilities for ablutions. Gas lighting in all dormitories. That'll do us fine, missus.'

There was a meal of cold roast beef and boiled mutton,

with pickles, bread and fruit pies, but Elizabeth was far too excited to eat more than a mouthful. It felt strange sleeping in the large crowded dormitory, full of people like them, here in London for the first time, all whispering in the dark about how excited they were about what lay ahead.

The next morning the Swifts dressed and readied themselves bright and early and set off for Hyde Park. All the omnibuses heading in that direction were overcrowded so they proceeded on foot. It was under a mile, but already the elastic around the satin shoes was cutting into the flesh of Elizabeth's feet and the back of the shoes were starting to chafe against her heels. She told herself not to think about it. Once she'd worn them in a bit they'd loosen up.

The roads were thronged with people. There were street traders everywhere: hawkers with trays containing miniature models of the Crystal Place, boys pushing barrows laden with nuts and baskets of oranges, or pushing carts selling ginger beer for a penny, while huge Union flags hung from the windows of public houses. As they entered the park there it was – the great glass building. A colossus towering over them, the sunlight shimmering through it, so that despite its enormous proportions, it seemed a light and airy creation, made of ice rather than iron and glass. The sign outside proudly proclaimed *The Great Exhibition of the Works of Industry and Art of All Nations*.

When they'd paid their shilling entrance fee, they went inside to a world that bedazzled them. The glass palace was so vast that it had swallowed up several of the elm trees of the park, now growing inside the building and dwarfed by its mammoth proportions.

'John, can you believe it? That there are men clever enough to make a building as huge as this one - you could fit Garswood Hall in here several times over!'

'There's no end to the invention of mankind, dearest. I

can honestly say I've never before felt so proud to be part of the Empire.'

They walked the length of the building, fascinated by everything they saw from the carpets and tapestries to the dental equipment and printing presses, from the giant Egyptian pharaohs to the steam turbines and the Jacquard lace machines. But no matter how impressed she was by the wonders around her, Elizabeth could think of nothing but the pain in her feet. By now she was limping badly, the bunions of thirty-six Lancastrian winters pressing against the cotton lining of the flimsy, satin shoes, the soles of her feet separated from the hard ground by a wafer-thin sole. The tiny feet that had slipped so easily into those shoes on her wedding day, had spread after eighteen years of married life and hard work. She was no longer a pretty, young bride. She limped on, cursing her vanity and stupidity and wishing she'd listened to her husband's advice. But she was too proud to say anything and besides, what good would it do now?

She trudged along behind John, increasingly oblivious to the wonders about them, thinking only how she had outgrown her shoes. Here she was now, mother to eight children, careworn, stout and spreading around the waist. John, though, was as handsome as he was the day he had asked her to marry him. She wished she had never had the crazy idea of coming on this adventure. All it had done was make her bunions worse. She looked around at the crowds of people. So many elegant women. What did he see in a fat old thing like her? This trip would be bound to make him discontent with his lot.

At last they stopped for a pot of tea in the refreshment court beside the great iron gates from Coalbrookdale. She sipped her tea, grateful to be seated at last, surreptitiously slipping off the shoes, out of sight under the table and wiggling her toes, curling and stretching them. Such freedom! Her soles tingled with a new kind of pain – an exquisite one, a blessed release, a tingling sensation.

A fountain tinkled away and the sounds of violin music played beyond the palm trees that surrounded the refreshment area. Elizabeth would have happily stayed there all day but John was already itching to see the latest advances in cotton spinning machinery. She rammed her feet back into the shoes, wincing with pain. A blister as well. She bit her lip and stood up. The brief respite had allowed her feet to swell and the shoes were tighter than ever. Cutting in. Burning. Searing pain. There was even a spot of blood on the cream satin. She fought back her tears. It was no good. She'd have to swallow her pride and ask John to take her back to the lodgings.

'Oh, John, I'm so sorry. You were quite right about the shoes. I should never have worn them. I cannot walk another step. I should have listened to you. What am I to do?'

He took her hand and led her back to the seat. From the depths of the pockets of his voluminous, caped greatcoat he pulled out first one and then the other of her battered, old, brown shoes. Without a word, he knelt on the ground in front of her and slipped them onto her swollen feet.

# THE PROPOSAL

## LIVERPOOL, 1934

*R*ita's eyes were still red raw from crying. She told her sister she hadn't slept all night, but it wasn't true. If she'd been awake she would have heard her father going downstairs, heard the creak of the rocking chair in the back kitchen, the sound of the conversation he'd had with her mother when she found him down there, and the whistle of the kettle as her mother made him a brew when he wouldn't come back to bed.

No, Rita had been oblivious to what was going on in the house while she slept a deep and undisturbed sleep, despite the damp pillow and swollen eyelids.

When she made her way downstairs that morning, her father had already left. To get picked for a shift on the docks you had to be there before seven. Rita poured herself a cup of tea and sat down at the table. She wrinkled her nose at the smell of burnt toast.

'You've a face on ya like a busted cabbage and your eyes are all puffed up,' said her sister, Katie. 'You should put some cucumber on them.'

Rita scowled. She'd been hoping it wasn't noticeable and anyway she knew there was no cucumber in the house.

'What's the matter? You been crying?'

'Leave her alone,' said their mother, knowing that Rita was never at her best in the morning.

But Katie was not easily rebuffed. 'What were you and Father arguing about last night? I heard you going at it like hammer and tongs after I'd gone to bed.'

'Well if you heard, what are you asking for?' Rita snapped. 'Leave me alone.' She flung down her half-eaten piece of toast and left the room. After a few moments they heard the front door slam.

'She's gone without me,' said Katie, stating the obvious.

Her mother shook her head with a look of resignation. 'Better to let Rita be on her own when she's like that. You can get the next tram. Enjoy a bit of peace before you get into work.' Susan O'Hara smiled at her younger daughter and shook her head. 'You know our Rita, once she's caught up with everything going on at the store she'll soon cheer up.'

Katie nodded. 'That's true. She's got a lot of interviews to do today. And the staff rotas. No time for moping.'

She looked at her mother and saw she hadn't touched her breakfast. 'What's wrong, Mother? You look so tired. Aren't you feeling well?'

'I'm grand,' her mother replied in her heavy Irish brogue, the tension lines on her forehead belying the statement.

'Is it because of Rita? She threw a right old paddy last night. I could hear her and Da arguing away but he wouldn't let me in the room.'

Katie could always be relied on to know exactly what was what. Nothing that happened in their small terraced house escaped her attention.

Susan O'Hara stared out of the window and sighed, then said, 'That fellow Rita was seeing last year – the one who went off to Canada and broke her heart – well he's written her a letter asking her to marry him.'

Katie gasped. 'Michael Maloney? Thanks be to God. That's marvellous. He's such a handsome fellow. So why the red eyes this morning and all the shouting last night?'

'Your father's told her she can't marry him.'

'Why not? He knows she's mad for him.'

'Well it's not that he's against her marrying him, but he says if Michael's serious about it, then he must come back to Liverpool and ask her properly.'

'Isn't that what he was always going to do? Come back here and get married and then take her back to Canada with him?'

'Apparently not.' Susan's voice was barely a whisper and her eyes were sad. 'Michael wants her to sail out there herself. Doesn't think it's worth paying for a ticket to come back over here to fetch her, when they'll need every penny they can find to set up home. And he says it would mean giving up his job. The Depression's as bad over there as it is here and he doesn't want to take the risk. He's got it all worked out.'

'I suppose I can see his point. You don't walk away from a good job.'

'Your Da knows that more than most but it's about the principle. Said that Michael Maloney was being disrespect-ful. No decent man would expect his wife-to-be to travel all the way to Canada on her own.'

'But, Mother, it's 1934. Times are changing.'

'Your father knows what goes on on ships. He wants to protect Rita.'

'He only knows about merchant ships. She'd be on a passenger liner. There'd be plenty of other women. They have separate quarters on board and it's all very respectable. Look at Theresa Connolly up the road, she works as a cabin steward for the White Star and she's back and forth to America all the time. No one says she's not respectable – her brother's a priest and two of her sisters are nuns.' She frowned. 'Can't you talk to Father. Make him think again?'

'I'll not go against your Da. He always knows best.'

'So what'll Rita do?' Katie scraped some stray toast crumbs into a pile on the tablecloth.

'Says she's going anyway. Even if Father disowns her. She's upset and angry and accused your father of wanting her to be an old maid.' She sighed deeply.

'She's already an old maid – she's twenty-five' said Katie. 'You weren't even eighteen when you married Father.'

'That was in Ireland. I think over here it's a bit different. There's plenty more fellas than that Michael Maloney.' Susan O'Hara got up from the table and began to clear away the dishes. 'A fine-looking girl like Rita. She can do much better. I always thought that Michael was shifty. Not to be trusted. He'd sell ya the eye outta ya head. Father thinks so too. That's why he's put his foot down. Rita will find someone else. Half the young men in the parish are chasing after her. She can take her pick.'

'Maybe she can. But perhaps she doesn't want to. She's mad for love of that fellow.'

Her mother leaned down and put her hand on her daughter's. 'You're awful soft underneath, our Katie. Now, look at the time. You'll be late for work. Get on with you.'

~

RITA CHEERED up as soon as she got into work. She loved working at Woolies. She was good at her job and the girls all looked up to her. They called her Miss O'Hara in the store and it made her feel important. Katie worked at Woolies too. They called her Miss Katherine to her face, but Rita knew

11

they called her The Dragon behind her back. Funny how everyone was scared of Katie. She had an air of being fierce, but Rita knew she had a heart as big as the new Mersey Tunnel.

Another reason for feeling cheerful was that she knew now that Michael did love her after all. How could she have doubted him? But she had. All those months without hearing a word – but now he'd not only written but he'd asked her to marry him. She felt vindicated after all the terrible things Father had said about how he'd done a moonlight flit, when she'd known all along he was wanting to prove himself in Canada first. I'll pave the way, set up base, he'd said. Her father was being a spoilsport about it – he just didn't like to be proved wrong – but Rita knew he'd come round eventually. She'd always been able to wind him round her little finger.

~

THE SUPPLY of men needing work on the docks far exceeded the demand, even though the pay was paltry. There was always a crowd of more than a hundred men chasing fewer than twenty jobs. If Harry O'Hara positioned himself near enough to the front of the crowd he had a chance to catch the foreman's eye, he was sometimes picked, even though he was an outsider.

He'd had to get used to having to hustle like this to get work – it had once been well beneath his dignity, but after so long out of a job he'd had to swallow his pride. And it took some swallowing – he had been a master mariner who had captained merchant ships around the globe. It was the highest possible qualification for a seafarer, permitting him to captain any size of ship anywhere in the world. He would return from his voyages laden with exotic gifts for Susan and their girls and be treated as a man of standing by friends and neighbours. Then two years ago his already poor eyesight started to fail. Objects had become blurred and out of focus. The eye doctor told him it was a degenerative condition and there was no hope of improvement. Now he couldn't even get a job as a second officer. A keen eye was a prerequisite for a seaman, for picking out other ships, icebergs, whales, reefs and rocks, as well as poring over detailed charts. So he had been forced to resort to dock labouring. 1934 was not a good time for a man in his fifties to retrain for a new profession.

Today Harry was in luck. He was picked for a gang discharging grain and cotton from a steam ship at the Sandon dock. Not as good as loading – the pay was always higher for stowing cargo than for taking it off, but better than going home empty-handed as had happened the previous day. No matter how long Harry O'Hara laboured on the docks he couldn't help his resentment that not so long ago he was in charge of ships bigger than this one and delegating the supervision of loading and discharge to the junior officers. Now he was one of the faceless mob of lumpers paid next to nothing to do hard labour.

He knew none of the gang he'd be working with – but then he never tried to ingratiate himself with the other workers, still harbouring the belief that he shouldn't be there rubbing shoulders with the likes of them. None of the rank and file workers had contracted jobs. Like Harry, they turned up and hoped for the best to be picked, even if sometimes it was just for a few hours; otherwise they'd be returning home with empty pockets.

When the foreman climbed onto the top of a crate to pick his gang, the men jostled, pushed, pulled, jockeyed for position, elbowed each other out of the way, shouted, waved and did everything they could to attract his attention. Few were dock workers by choice. They were mostly men down on their luck, out of work, laid off from their chosen occupations, although, unlike Harry, none had had a profession. Among them was a smattering of habitual drunkards, jailbirds, injured and unfortunates, trying their luck. Harry, believing he would have nothing in common with any of them, kept himself to himself.

He joined the men on the deck of the ship and was assigned by the foreman to operate a fall, to discharge the cargo from the hull of the ship onto the dock below. It was hard work, piling up and roping the heavy sacks before attaching the big metal hooks so they could be winched down onto the dockside.

Harry was troubled. He hated conflict. His daughter Rita was headstrong. A beautiful girl; he was proud of her. When she'd left school she'd got herself a job in Woolworth's and had worked her way up to a position of responsibility, supervising the shop assistants. Her sister Katie had followed her and both were now doing well. It had made up for his guilt about dragging them over to Liverpool when his ships mainly sailed to and from here, rather than their hometown of Dublin. Otherwise he'd have rarely seen his family. While they all missed the fine townhouse they'd lived in back in Ireland, they'd made lives for themselves in more humble housing in Liverpool and he had been planning to buy a grander house, maybe in Southport or Crosby. But then his eyesight worsened and he had failed the required tests.

In bed the previous night, he had tossed and turned, anxious about Rita and whether he had been right to forbid her following that fella to Canada. He didn't want to alienate her. He loved that girl with all his heart and hated to deny her anything but Michael Maloney wasn't good enough for her. Worse, Harry suspected the reason for the fella shipping off to Canada in the first place was not to better himself but to escape trouble of some kind.

Susan had sensed his absence and came downstairs to ask him why he was unable to sleep.

'It's nothing, Sue, just a bad dream.'

'Is it the business with Rita?' she asked, laying her hand on his arm. 'Are ya thinking you were too hard on her?'

'No. She'll have forgotten that eejit by Christmas. Just as she did when he went off in the first place. She's just being wilful. Enjoying the attention. That's our Rita.' He'd tried to smile.

She looked at him and stroked his head with her hand. 'Perhaps it's best you stay at home today as you've missed your sleep. Don't go to work. You're dog-tired, Harry. That's what it is. We'll get by just for one day. Stay home and rest. That'll sort you out. Now I'm going to make you a nice cup of tea.'

But he hadn't listened to her. He'd had two days already this week with no work. If it weren't for the two girls working, they'd struggle to get by. His pride was wounded. He hated having to rely on his daughters to supplement the household income.

Harry felt bad. Had he behaved that way to Rita for selfish reasons? Was he only trying to keep her here because of her job? If she were to go to Canada they'd all feel the effect. Not to mention missing her. That was the worst part. Never to see his firstborn child again. He sighed and hauled the hook across the deck and attached it to another sack of grain.

Maybe he should think again? Give the Maloney lad another chance. He could write to him and let him know his misgivings and see how the fellow responded. It would buy more time. Time for Rita to meet another fellow. One from the parish who wasn't going to gallivant across the Atlantic seeking his fortune. He wouldn't mention that part to Rita though. He'd merely stress the importance of Maloney explaining himself. After all, Rita had looked nonplussed when he had asked whether her fella intended to pay for her ticket.

~

RITA FINISHED the last of a series of interviews with young women applying to work in the store. Smiling brightly, she ushered the last candidate out of her tiny office. There was always a plentiful supply of girls keen to secure a job in Woolworth's. Liverpool was Woolie's number one store, the jewel in the retailer's crown. Shop work was about the only work, apart from nursing, that women were welcome in these days – since the war and the depression the priority was getting men into paid work. Not for the first time Rita told herself how lucky she was.

She thought about how her father had refused to give his permission for her to marry Michael. He was so old fashioned. So stubborn. He just didn't want her to be happy. It wasn't fair. She had such a fancy for Michael Maloney. The way he looked at her always made her tummy do somersaults – that slightly sly, appraising look as though he was thinking about what he'd like to do to her when they were married. Thinking of it now made her feel all hot and bothered.

Rita picked up the pile of job applications from her desk and divided them into three smaller piles – the yeses, who would get a trial period in the store, the maybes, who would be kept in reserve, and the no's, who already had a big cross through their forms. She filed the maybes and the no's in the wooden filing cabinet and put the yeses on one side.

It was hard to picture Michael's face. She could remember his expression and how it made her feel, but his features had become hard to recall, as it was months since she'd seen him. An awfully handsome fellow though. Everyone thought that. And he had chosen her.

Her brow furrowed as she realised she would have to give up her job at Woolies. Give up the status and respect it afforded her; lose the money it brought her – and the things she was able to buy herself after her contribution to the household expenses. Rita loved clothes. Hats particularly. And her regular trips to the shoe shop. Goodness – there might not even be a shoe shop where she was going in Canada. Before long she'd have a houseful of babies and her time would be spent washing and ironing. No more dancing. No more trips to New Brighton and holidays on the Welsh coast. No more parish outings. She didn't even know where she would be living. It might be in the middle of nowhere. What did she know of Canada anyway? Michael had given her no details.

Rita squeezed her lips, remembering what her father had pointed out – that Michael hadn't even sent her the ticket. She'd have to find the money for the passage herself. It would blow all her savings.

The door of her office opened and her friend Jean put her head around it. 'Coming to the dance tonight, Rita?'

Without a moment's hesitation, Rita said, 'I wouldn't miss it for the world.'

∼

THE WINCH OPERATOR HAD DISAPPEARED. Harry suspected a few of them were throwing numbers. The man had been going off for a few minutes, without explanation, every half hour or so, out of sight behind the bales of cotton and Harry could hear groans of disappointment and triumphant laughter as they spun the dice. Gambling on the job was strictly forbidden. He was tempted to tell the ship's officer, but that would win him no friends and probably cost him in the future. Besides, what did he owe the captain? He clearly didn't run a tight ship. Harry would never have let that kind of thing happen under his command. A surge of anger rose in him. Damn his eyesight.

He moved back across the deck as the winch lifted the sacks of grain. That fellow had left the machinery running, unsupervised. Another thing that was against all the rules. He was about to call out to him to turn it off, as the load had already landed on the dockside, when he slipped.

It happened so quickly. The deck was wet from a rain shower earlier that morning, and the husks from the grain made it slippery under his feet. The thought that he should have got his shoes repaired flashed through his head as he fell, then his body was caught up in an agony of tightening wire and crushed bone, as he was trapped in the steel cable of the winch and wound around the drum.

The other lumpers heard his screams and ran to switch the machinery off, but by then he was halfway round the drum. They laid his crushed and mangled body upon the deck. Harry breathed a couple of tortured breaths and his eyes blinked as though trying to take in what had happened to him then, in a explosion of shock and pain, his heart stopped.

~

WHEN KATIE and Rita got off the tram, they were full of excitement about the dance they were going to that night and what they were going to wear. They rounded the corner to their own street and stopped short in surprise. A crowd of women were filling up the road and most of the front doors stood open.

'What's going on? Looks like something's happened.'

The sisters walked into the crowd. As the bystanders saw them, they went quiet and stepped aside to clear a path for the two women to their own front door, the only one in the street that wasn't wide open.

Outside the house, the parish priest was waiting. He put his hands on their shoulders and drew them close.

'I've very sad news for you, girls. Your poor father was killed on the docks today. I need you to be strong for your mother. She's still at the hospital. She has to identify him. Molly Mason has gone with her. Oh, girls, you can be sure they will have a very big seat for Harry O'Hara up in heaven. Right next to Our Blessed Lady.'

Rita's legs gave way and she stumbled but Katie caught her. She wanted to cry but the tears wouldn't come. Instead she felt a numbness inside, an emptiness, a grief that she knew would never wholly leave her.

'My last words to him were said in anger. God, forgive me.' Her voice was barely a whisper.

The only obstacle to her marrying Michael Maloney was gone, but she knew she would never go to Canada now.

# THE SOUND OF SILENCE

## ENGLAND, TODAY

The sun lit up the clay tiles on the cottage roof, suffusing them with a rosy glow against the peacock blue sky. A perfect day. Gemma pulled onto the driveway, heart racing, unable to stop grinning. Yes, the garden was more overgrown than when she'd last visited and the loose guttering the surveyor had pointed out in the home buyer's report, was now dangling away from the eaves. And yes, it had been a struggle to make up the deposit and negotiate the mortgage while her solicitor had debated what seemed to her trivial issues with the vendors' solicitors. But at last she was here.

She'd done it. Her very own place for the first time in her thirty-six years. The honeysuckle and roses rambling around the front door were straight off the lid of an old fashioned chocolate box. She hugged herself and gave a little joyful skip as she fished in her handbag for the keys.

The cottage looked sad and bare inside, the walls marked with pale squares where the former owners' pictures had hung. The kitchen floor tiles were dirty and there were dense cobwebs on the wall and skirting where the fridge had once stood. The living room carpet was badly stained. The previous owners had covered it with a rug so she hadn't noticed the marks during her two brief viewings. Upstairs, the bedroom floors were littered with abandoned metal coat hangers. She found a sock draped over one of the radiators and a stray pair of underpants in the airing cupboard.

All that scrubbing and cleaning she'd done before vacating the house in Hammersmith, only to be faced with this. Why had she bothered? Pride, she supposed. Stupid really, as she'd never even met her buyers. She'd had to manage the sale and removal on her own as Charlie wouldn't lift a finger to help her. By the time it came to clearing everything out, the divorce lawyers had done so much damage to the few remaining threads of their marriage that they couldn't bear to be in the same room with each other.

Gemma set about cleaning up the cottage before the removal men arrived. Charlie had claimed most of the furniture and she had retained only the few things she had brought into the marriage with her from her five years in a rented flat. She wanted none of the items they had chosen together. They would have reminded her of him and of the marriage that had started off in hope and harmony and then curdled like sour milk.

When the removal men had left and she had arranged things as best she could and made a list of stuff she needed to buy for the cottage, she dragged a chair outside into the small garden and sat in the receding daylight with a glass of red wine. The sun set in a blood-red burst behind the hills and the air was filled with the scent of nicotiana and phlox that bordered the tiny lawn. For a moment Gemma felt perfectly happy, content – at home.

The evening air chilled and she cursed that she had forgotten to order logs for the wood burning stove. Shivering, she lit a few candles and looked around, appraising her efforts and making mental notes for tomorrow's tasks. After a leisurely candlelit bath, she headed up to bed, satisfied with her day and excited about her future in her new home.

It was strange trying to sleep in new surroundings. She felt disorientated. There was the added strangeness of sleeping in her old bed from her rented flat – it had been exiled to the guest room in Hammersmith and Gemma remembered why now, as she experienced the hard profiles of the wooden slats through the thin mattress, like the princess and the pea. She had expected to go off to sleep straight away, as she always did – even at the height of her battles with Charlie. When she was a child her mother used to laugh at the way she was asleep as soon as her head touched the pillow. But not tonight. Her first night in her new home plagued by insomnia. A double first.

After lying awake for what seemed like hours in the dark silent room, she began to feel afraid. She got out of bed and went to look out of the uncurtained window. Her eyes took a few moments to adjust to the almost impenetrable darkness. Nothing there – just the black bulk of elm trees looming over the curve of bushes and shrubs in the front garden and the dark shape of her car on the drive. No moon. No street lamps. Silence. Unearthly silence. Impenetrable. Eerie.

She climbed back into bed. She wanted to turn on the radio to break the silence but inexplicably felt more afraid of the sound of voices penetrating the quiet. Why? It was as if there was something or someone there inside the house and switching on the radio would make this "presence" aware that she was there too. Ridiculous. She shivered underneath the heavy duvet and looked at the time on the illuminated fascia of her alarm clock. Well into the World Service by this time. Still she hesitated.

Lying in the uncomfortable bed she gazed unseeing into the dark, paralysed with fear. She could hear the sound of her heart beating in her chest and knew that whatever or whoever was there in the dark silent house would hear it too.

The cottage adjoined another on one side but the estate agent had stressed that the walls being several feet thick, there was no risk of neighbour noise problems. No risk of anyone hearing if she cried out for help either.

She wanted to go to the bathroom but was too frightened to move. Telling herself not to be so crazy she stretched out her hand to the bedside lamp. The click of the switch made her jump and she recoiled with shock as the light from the weak energy-saving bulb seemed to fill up the room like Blackpool Illuminations. The bathroom was downstairs and she flinched at every creak of the bare oak stairs as she made her way down there. She was too afraid to flush the toilet, fearing the explosion of sound breaking through the solid wall of silence.

Back in bed she told herself that this was normal first night nerves, but she wasn't making a very good job of convincing herself. Maybe leaving London was not as good an idea as it had seemed.

By the time morning came, Gemma was exhausted and spaced-out, as though she had awoken from an anaesthetic after a major operation. She made a cup of tea and sat in her pyjamas on the back doorstep, looking out at the sun-filled cottage garden watching a bird pecking at the shell of a snail.

In the radiance of the morning, her night fears seemed implausible, but she still felt uneasy. Driving off to shop for the items on her list, she found herself steering the car in the opposite direction - towards the motorway and back to London.

A couple of hours later she was knocking at the front door of her friend's flat. Steph worked from home and could usually be relied upon to be in and ready for an excuse to down tools and put the kettle on.

'I've made a terrible mistake. I think the cottage is haunted. What am I going to do? I can't possibly live there.'

Steph laughed. 'Come on, Gem, every old cottage feels haunted. That's half the attraction. You know, imagining who's lived there before you. All those unknown people. All those hopes and dreams and fears and sorrows.' She handed her a cup of coffee. 'Not surprising that it should feel a bit weird at first. You'll soon get used to it.'

'Cheers. That's made me feel better. NOT. Now I'll lie in bed worrying about whether someone was murdered and their spirit has been left behind.'

'For God's sake, woman, pull yourself together. Tell me exactly what happened. What did you see? What did you hear? What spooked you? '

Gemma hesitated. 'That's just it. Nothing.'

'Nothing?' Stephanie raised an eyebrow. 'And you've driven all the way back here to tell me that!'

'I know it sounds barmy but it was the silence. And the dark. Completely dark. Terrifyingly dark.'

'Get a night light.' Stephanie laughed. 'My Mum used to keep a red bulb burning day and night under her statue of the Sacred Heart of Jesus. Maybe you should get one. That should keep the ghosts away! Or you could get a priest round and do an exorcism.'

'Please, Steph, stop taking the piss. I'm serious. It's so scary. Total silence and total dark. I could hear my own blood pumping'

Steph frowned, then put her mug down and took her by the arm and led her outside into the small back yard that passed for a garden at this end of Hammersmith.

'Shut your eyes. Now I want you to listen. And I mean really listen. I'm going to put the kettle on again and then you can tell me everything you've heard and we can have another chat about your ghostly country cottage.'

Slightly bewildered, but accustomed to Steph's frequent obtuseness, Gemma stood, eyes tightly closed, and listened to the sounds that were so familiar she had never really heard them before.

The police sirens played a strident symphony, starting as a low whistle and screaming as they came nearer, then fading, followed by another siren rising and falling on a different pitch. The receding throb of a jet moving through the skies towards Heathrow. A hammer hitting wood and the metallic thump of a heavy object. Probably something landing in one of the many skips that lined the street. A few houses away, the clatter of cutlery taken out of a dishwasher and dropped into a drawer. The throaty roar of another jet. Why had she always maintained the complaints about aircraft noise were exaggerations? Somewhere close by, a door slammed. A baby cried and was drowned out by the screams of another child, as a motorbike roared down the street, braking hard at the junction. Underneath it all she began to make out the constant threnody of traffic on the A4. Another siren – surely there wasn't that much crime around here? Voices speaking a foreign language and the tinny tones of a transistor radio on some electro dance channel - Polish builders. An oven timer pinged and the wind chimes in the next door garden rattled an echoing tune.

She felt a hand on her arm.

'So?' Stephanie handed her a mug of coffee.

'It's so noisy here. How come I never noticed before? How did I stand it? How do you?'

'You never listened. We all tune it out, or else we'd go mad!'

'But there's so much. The planes! The sirens!'

'Look, none of us would stand it if we did what you just did - really listened and paid attention. You never heard it when you were living here. But you missed it without even knowing that you did, last night.' She sipped her coffee and smiled at Gemma. 'That's your ghost – the Ghost of London Lost!'

'So it's just a case of getting used to the sound of silence?'

'Do what you just did now when you get home. I bet if you really listen properly, you'll start to hear things even in the quiet of the country night.'

~

THAT NIGHT GEMMA lay in her bed and listened to the wind rustling the leaves in the elm trees as she reminded herself to order a new mattress. In the distance she made out what she guessed was the scream of a fox. Eyes closed, she heard the low faraway rumble of a goods train travelling along the railway that passed half a mile from the village, before she fell into a deep and undisturbed asleep.

# THE PERUVIAN HAT

## PARIS

'*I*t's bloody freezing. I don't think I've ever felt so cold before.' Anna stamped her feet in the snow. 'I thought it wasn't supposed to snow in Paris.'

'Let's go to a museum? It's bound to be warmer inside.' Marissa always tried to solve problems. It was one of her most irritating habits. When all Anna wanted was a bit of sympathy or a shoulder to cry on, Marissa would offer a plan of action designed to make everything all right. What was wrong with having a good moan and a bit of wallowing every now and then?

'I'd rather walk around and soak up the atmosphere in the streets. But my ears feel as though someone's poking icicles through them.'

'In that case you need a hat.' Marissa pointed to her own hand knitted beanie. 'I'm lovely and warm. Well – apart from my nose. I think that's about to turn black and drop off.' She laughed. 'Let's go and find you one.'

She grabbed Anna's arm and hauled her along the pavement. 'I'm sure I saw a load of stalls selling clothing down here last night.' She pointed in the direction of the Place St Germain. 'You're bound to find a bargain.'

'I hate hats.' Anna was feeling grumpy and wanting to resist Marissa's determination to fix things.

Marissa grinned. 'That's a barefaced lie. You love them.'

'No I don't.'

'Then shut up and freeze. You're not having mine.'

Anna scowled and followed her friend towards the group of street stalls which were doing a brisk trade in scarves, gloves and hats for the freezing tourists. She made a beeline for a stand full of Peruvian knitted hats – the kind with generous earflaps and little dangling plaits. She picked one up and tried it on, looking around for a means of seeing what it looked like. The stall holder produced a small mirror and Anna studied her reflection. 'I've always hankered after one of these. What do you think?'

'It suits you. Looks warm too.'

'Warm as toast. It's got a flannel lining. My ears might actually defrost in this! Shall I?'

'Yes buy it. It's cute.'

'You don't think I'm too old for it?'

'Don't be daft. Anyone can wear one of them. Old Peruvian ladies of about a hundred wear them. It's probably why they live so long and survive the high altitudes,' said Marissa.

'You do talk a load of crap sometimes!' She turned to the stallholder. '*Je le prend*.'

Ignoring her attempt at French, the man said in English, 'You want it? Ten euros.'

The hat firmly on her head, Anna stuffed her hands in her pockets and set off with renewed energy. 'Let's walk through the Latin Quarter and cross over to the Isle St Louis. We can have a mooch around the little shops over there and grab another coffee, then head to the Marais.'

They walked through the streets of the left bank, which

were blanketed in unfamiliar snow, chatting and looking in shop windows. They strolled along a narrow street, lined with shops selling antiques and fine paintings. There was hardly anyone about, as though the Parisian population had wisely decided to spend the weekend indoors rather than venturing into the icy city.

A young man walked towards them, tall, with an athletic build. Anna looked at him as he approached, taking in his handsome face and trying not to wish she was twenty years younger. He was wearing a Peruvian hat just like hers and she felt a little flutter of pleasure at discovering a kindred spirit. It was as if they were in an exclusive club. She gave him a little conspiratorial smile as they passed.

She didn't know what made her turn around to look after him. Perhaps it was the hope that he would be doing the same and looking wistfully after her. She was just in time to see him jerk the hat off his head and drop it into a litter bin.

# THE GLASS OF MILK

## 1948

*J*ean looked inside her purse again. Surely there must be a penny or two? Maybe a coin had slipped under the lining? But the cotton interior was still intact despite the age of the purse and the scuffed exterior, Nothing. She went through her coat pockets and rummaged inside her battered handbag. Not a brass farthing.

Archie didn't get paid until tomorrow so it wouldn't be until he came home at lunchtime that she'd have any money at all. What was she to do? Not even enough cash for a pint of milk and she'd die before asking the grocer for tick. Archie would go mad if she did that. You'll make a holy show of us he'd surely say. He liked to think that as a teacher he had a reputation to uphold and as a professional should be a cut above the kind of people who needed to rely on tick to get through a week till payday.

Thank goodness she still had some leftover stew. She'd managed to stretch that over three nights. She felt bad serving such skinny portions to Archie with him working hard all day at school. He needed food to feed his brain and give him the energy to ride that bike up the long hill home at the end of the day.

Her own upbringing hadn't prepared her for this life. There had never been any shortage of food at home. But when she'd agreed to marry Archie Walton she'd known what she was letting herself in for. She'd known that a teacher's pay didn't compare with her father's salary as a bank manager. At the time she hadn't cared. She was heedless that she'd be living in a simple terraced house without a refrigerator or a decent cooker – and anyway she'd managed fine on the Baby Belling. Jean loved Archie and that was all that mattered.

But since the war, rationing was as hard as ever and on top of that there had been cutback after cutback and teachers were no different from anyone else. Everyone had to make sacrifices. It was just that no one expected the sacrifices to go on year after year. Jean had thought that having fought and won a war they were entitled to enjoy the peace but it didn't seem to work that way. Archie had tried to explain why, but his talk of economics, national debt and unemployment had her eyes glazing over. She had to acknowledge that having a poorly paid job was better than no job at all and compared with others, they were well off. But it was still hard for her to get used to this constant struggle to make ends meet.

She glanced up at the clock. Archie would be home soon. She laid the table and put the pan of stew on to simmer. It didn't look much. She'd just have to plead a poor appetite and give Archie most of her share. At least she never had to worry about her waistline. She peeled and quartered the last of the potatoes and dumped them into the stew with a bit of extra water, another pinch of salt and a shake of pepper. Her stomach rumbled.

She flicked the wireless on. She liked to listen to a play or story on the Home Service before Children's Hour at five.

They were serialising Great Expectations at the moment and she didn't want to miss it.

Just as the music for Children's Hour came on, the back door opened and Archie came into the room, his face lit up by a huge grin. Jean flicked off the wireless. He didn't stop to take off his bicycle clips but picked her up and twirled her around the kitchen, narrowly avoiding knocking the pan off the stove.

He put her down and bent to kiss her. 'How was your day, Jeanie, my love?'

She returned the kiss, before moving back to the cooker to stir the stew, trying not to let the rumbling in her stomach give her away. Smiling at him she answered. 'Oh same old stuff. You know. Housework. A cup of tea at Mrs Oliver's as I promised to look in her now her daughter is away. She gets very lonely you know.'

'What did I do to deserve a wife like you? Big hearted as well as beautiful.' He moved behind her and put his arms around her waist and leaned his head against her neck as she stirred the pot. He breathed in and said, 'Mmm. Smells delicious. Not only have I the kindest and most caring of wives, I have the best cook into the bargain.'

'It's just the same stew you had last night.' Her voice was apologetic. 'Nothing to get excited about.'

'It's manna from heaven to me.'

'You're daft, you are,' she said, grinning at him. 'Sit down and I'll serve up and you can tell me about school. How was *your* day?'

'Not much to report. That kid I told you about last week, you know – the one who told the school inspector she liked baking bread as it made her hands lovely and clean...'

Jean laughed and gave a little shudder. 'Yes, if she brings a loaf in for teacher, don't even think about bringing it home!'

'Well, today the doctor was in doing a health check for

the new National Health Service. All the children had to take their shirts and vests off so he could listen to their chests with his stethoscope. He got to her and she was still fully dressed. "Take your clothes off, lassie,' he said. And she said. 'Sorry. mister I can't. Me Mam's sewn me in for the winter." Can you believe it!'

Jean laughed then shook her head. "We shouldn't be laughing. It's terrible the way some people have to live.' She handed him his plate of stew and sat down with hers. She'd spread the watery concoction around the plate in the hope that he wouldn't notice her scant portion.

'You don't seem to have a lot on your plate.'

'I've already had some. I kept dipping the spoon in the pot while it was cooking. I know I should have waited but I couldn't resist.'

He smiled at her and reached for his glass of milk, holding it up to toast her health. He waited for her to chink her glass against his then saw that she was drinking water, not milk.

'Now my dear heart, I must take you to task,' he said. 'I have such a hard job keeping you on the straight and narrow and I don't know how I'm going to lick you into shape!'

'What do you mean?' Jean spluttered her water in surprise.

'You're a very bad girl. Whenever the milk is running a little low my glass always manages to be fuller than yours. Now for the sake of marital harmony and to avoid your inevitable protests, I have born this stoically and in silence. But tonight my darling you've gone too far.'

'What on earth are you talking about?'

Archie pointed to her glass of water. 'I'm talking about that! Have you gone teetotal all of a sudden? Switched from the bounty of the cow to Adam's Ale?'

'I don't feel a bit like milk tonight,' she said, taking another sip of her water.

Archie put his glass down. 'Now tell me the truth, love of my life, is there any more milk in the house?'

'No,' Jean said, 'which is just as well as I don't feel like drinking milk tonight.'

'That's a strange coincidence, as I don't feel like it either.' He pushed his glass towards her.

'Now don't you go playing the fool with me, Archie Compton. 'Cut that out or I'll be vexed.'

'In that case. No milk for Jean, no milk for Archie,' he said, leaning back in his chair and giving her a pantomime frown.

Jean scowled back at him.

'Will you have half?' he asked.

'I told you I don't want milk. If the house was full of milk I shouldn't drink a drop and I won't have your milk so it's final.' She folded her arms.

'In that case, I'll have water too.' Archie got up from the table, took a clean glass from the cupboard and went towards the sink.

'You brute!' Jean cried. You bully! Making me drink milk against my will.' She tried not to laugh as she poured half of Archie's milk into the empty glass.

Archie moved the glass of milk towards his mouth and took a mouthful then spat it out on the tablecloth. Jean jumped in surprise.

'You fiendish creature! It's sour as blazes! Practically cheese.'

'I'm sorry, my love,' she said. 'I didn't realise it had gone off.' She started to giggle. 'I'd have shared my glass of water with you had I known.'

Archie burst out laughing and reached across the table and took her hand in his.

# SURVIVAL

## SOMEWHERE IN THE USA, TODAY

*T*he Kindle hit the wall of the trailer, bounced off and landed in the overflowing cat litter tray.

'Filth!' she screamed.

Lifting her bulk out of the La-Z-Boy chair, Betty-Sue slumped onto her knees and began to pray out loud, her voice strident as she begged the Lord to bring down curses and the foulest punishments of hell upon the woman who had written the book she had just read.

As she spoke the words in a wild incantation, she struggled to erase the memory of the story. Why had she kept on reading? Why hadn't she stopped and saved her mind from being polluted by the words on the page? But $2.99 was $2.99 and she'd wanted her money's worth. These were hard times – even for the righteous.

And the book had been a page turner, impossible to give up on the story once it had hooked her in. The true work of the devil. That's how he got you. Sucked you in with words and stories that gripped you so tight you couldn't stop reading until it was too late. She reached for the bible and read a few verses out loud, hoping to banish any lingering traces of the evil she had allowed to enter her home.

The novel had been set at the turn of the twentieth century, so it was perfectly reasonable to expect a tale about good people doing good things. In those days folk observed the sanctity of marriage, understood sexual relations were only for procreation and were God-fearing, church-going people. But this author had tricked her. Lulled her into a false sense of security then unleashed the demons of sinfulness upon her, like the plagues of Egypt.

The book had started off so well – a young girl, tragically orphaned, working as a governess. What could be purer than that? She had read on in the expectation that the heroine, who was even named after a Biblical character, would marry and live happily ever after. But no – not only did she become an adulteress, she performed her disgusting acts of fornication with a clergyman,, tempting this man of God like the Jezebel she should have been named. Another character had had a child out of wedlock with hints that it might have been sired by her father. Incest. Filth. Filth. Filth.

Betty-Sue felt dirty, contaminated, unclean. She wanted to pour bleach over her Kindle. But that would be wasteful. She'd paid good money for it.

She heaved herself to her feet, shuffling her bulk across the floor, weaving unsteadily between the pizza boxes, the cats and the beer cans. Must get that son of hers to clear up after himself. Why did he never listen to her? Every step was painful, her inner thighs chafing against each other and the lycra of her leggings. She forced a hand between her legs. Another hole in the fabric. Betty-Sue got through joggers and leggings faster than a tube of Pringles.

She leaned down, gasping for breath at the effort, and plucked her Kindle from the litter tray, brushing off the cat waste with her fat fingers. Passing the fridge, she leaned in and took a can of diet soda and staggered back to her chair, lifting one of the cats onto her knee. Ten minutes later she had removed all trace of the offending novel from the device. If only she could remove it so easily from her head.

Glancing at her cellphone, Betty-Sue saw it was nearly eleven. Clayton ought to be home by now. And that son of theirs too. But Bobby-Ray was out more than he was in these days. And him only sixteen. She despaired about how to keep that boy on the path of righteousness. She kept on at Clayton to take a belt to him. Knock a bit of sense into the kid, but he always seemed to have other things on his mind and kept telling her to give the boy a break.

Betty-Sue didn't like to cross Clayton. He had a temper on him when he'd had a few drinks. Not that he did that every night. He was a good man was Clayton. Always did the right thing. Hadn't he stood by her through thick and thin, good times and bad? Even if they did get off on the wrong foot – he put things right eventually. When she'd first met him he was a good-looking man. Still was, in her eyes, even if he had a bit of a belly nowadays. But who was she to talk? She'd put on a few pounds over the years herself. Well, more than a few if she was honest, but she wasn't going to have one of those gastric bands fitted, like the doc suggested. No siree. If she was a little on the curvy side it was because God intended it that way. Who was she to interfere with the ways of the good Lord? Besides they hadn't the money for surgery.

She reached out with her grabber stick and hauled an open box of Reece's peanut butter cups across the carpet and popped one in her mouth, Luxuriating in the sweet melting taste of peanut she reached for another before she had swallowed the first. Life had few enough pleasures after all.

Betty-Sue raised her eyes to the framed photograph on the trailer wall. She had been thin as a pin on her wedding day – apart from the bump in front and you couldn't see that head-on. Clayton had his eyes scrunched up tight, looking into the sun. He never did like having his picture taken. Betty-Sue smiled, remembering how her daddy had taken Clayton aside when he found out she was in the family way. She'd tried to listen through the wall but couldn't hear what they were saying. After that, Clayton stopped telling her they should wait to get to married and went right on out and booked the preacher for the following day. Daddy always had a powerful persuasive way about him.

After Bobby-Ray had come into the world, she and Clayton had a talk about having more children and decided that Bobby-Ray was all they needed. Clayton left her alone after that, praise the lord. He was indeed a righteous man. He turned his back on Satan and the temptations of the flesh. So what if he did spend too much time and too much money on liquor. A man deserved some pleasure in this world. Better that than messing around with women.

Her stomach cramped sharply and she felt a piercing stab of pain, like an electric shock in her belly. Where was the Pepto Bismol? She strained to pull herself upright onto her feet. Clayton had come in late the night before stinking of beer and she'd heard him fumbling around in the bathroom. She went in there now, holding onto the edge of the furniture as the cats rubbed up against her ankles. Not in the medicine chest. Only his shaving gear, about a year's supply of Tylenol, six bottles of Poo-Pourri Before-you-Go spray (on special in Walmart – shame Clayton never remembered to use it) and another box of peanut butter cups she'd hidden in there where Bobby-Ray wouldn't find them. The pain stabbed again and she slugged a couple of the Tylenol, pushing her head under the tap to wash them down.

Darn it – where was that Pepto Bismol? Where had Clayton put it? She looked around the living room. Every surface was covered with empty food cartons and cans. One of the cats jumped up on top of the sink drainer and she brushed it off. 'Gidd'out, Brandy!' she said. As the cat slunk away another jumped up and took its place and began licking the residues of spilt milk next to the empty cereal box on the counter. Betty-Sue shook her head. No point in bothering. Keeping the cats at bay was like that game of Wack-a-mole she used to play with Bobby-Ray before he decided such things were beneath his teenage dignity.

She went into the bedroom. Only Clayton slept in there. She preferred to stay in the La-Z-Boy herself as lying flat made her indigestion worse. It was his domain. Reaching up she opened the door of the cupboard that ran above the bed.

A pile of magazines tumbled out onto the bed. Betty Sue gathered the copies of Survivalist Monthly and stuffed them back into the cupboard. No sign of the PeptoBismol. She was about to head back to the comfort of the La-Z-Boy when she frowned. Something wasn't right. Going back into the living room she got her grabber and returned to the bedroom and pulled the magazines out of the cupboard. There in the middle of the "prepper"magazines was a glossy publication with well thumbed pages, some of which appeared to be stuck together. She pulled it towards her and looked at it in mounting horror. Pornography. The images were beyond anything Betty-Sue could imagine. Naked women on every page. Slim naked women. She felt the nausea rise in her throat. 'Filth!' she screamed again, her voice verging on hysteria.

~

CLAYTON HADLEY COULD BARELY FOCUS when he approached the front door of the trailer. The shots of bourbon on top of the beers had made him feel unsteady on his feet. He looked at the pathway in front of him. The descent to hell he called it. He'd already endured nearly seventeen years of what he saw as his sentence, but until Abner Denton was dead or infirm, he was tied to Betty-Sue Denton and tied to the miserable squalid life they shared in that trailer park. She'd been willing enough when he'd had her up against the barn door all those years ago. Not pretty, but not ugly either. And his philosophy had always been if a girl's putting out for you, what she looks like don't matter. But then as soon as she had a ring on her finger Betty-Sue had stopped putting out.

After a while Clayton hadn't cared any more. There were plenty of women in Haytown who'd be happy to give a man what he needed in exchange for a few beers and a bit of conversation. Over the years Betty-Sue had turned into a beached whale, so obese that she couldn't even get herself to church any more and just watched those preachers on the TV day and night. Even if she'd been willing, he wouldn't have been able to get it up for her. When she wasn't glued to the TV screen she had her head in her Kindle reading Christian romances and apocalypse stories, while waiting for the Rapture and stuffing her fat face with junk.

Ten years back he'd taken off; decided to go and live in the back woods and put his survivalist hobby to good use away from her toxic presence. Abner Denton had tracked him down and a shotgun in the face was still a powerful incentive to toe the line.

Opening the door, Clayton didn't have time to see Betty-Sue had a gun in her hands. Didn't spot the copy of Playboy magazine lying in shreds at her feet. Didn't even notice the powerful stench of bleach rising from the torn up pages.

Clayton slumped forward onto the floor, crushing an empty box of fried chicken pieces. His blood mingled with the contents of a spilt can of soda and soaked into the carpet.

'Filth!' she muttered. 'Filth.'

# A MOTHER'S LOVE

## 1793, SHOREHAM, ENGLAND

He was calling to her again. At first she thought it was just the wind screaming against the eaves of the cottage, but now she was certain it was her boy's voice, carried on the air by the gale. The old woman remembered his cries as a baby, often inconsolable – his lack of speech until five years old had made it hard for the child to let her know what ailed him. Then there had been her gradual realisation that James was never going to be like other children. He would always be slower: slow in movements and slower still to learn, to think. She had shuddered with fear for him when she accepted at last that he was what other folk called a simpleton. It had made her love for the boy fiercer. She was all he had. His father had died before the boy was born, leaving her alone to struggle, first to bring him into the world and then to bring him up. The terrible pain of her long, lonely labour had been worth it. At last, after years of barrenness, she was a mother, holding her own child in her arms, feeling him nuzzling and sucking at her breast, listening to his mewling and snuffling as he guzzled her milk like a hungry kitten, his skin warm against hers, his need for her absolute. That he was dull-witted, scrawny, a runt in her otherwise empty litter, made her love him all the more.

She scrabbled about in the dark of the one-room cottage to find her shawl. It was always best to go to him when it was night. Storms, wind and rain made it safer, less likely that she'd be spotted. She couldn't risk being seen. They'd stop her doing what she had to do. Her hand stroked the top of the old wooden chest that stood against the end of her bed. It was filling up and tonight she would have more to put inside it, God willing.

～

'YOU'RE A SCAREDY CHICKEN, you are, lad. Too daft to do anything that might be called dangerous.' The man leaned forward, grinning at James over the top of his tankard of ale. 'I knows you'd never dare do anything as might be reckoned to be against the law.'

James Rook was indignant. 'I'm as brave as anyone. Brave as a bear. Brave as...' He thought for a moment then said, 'a lion.'

'You've never seen a lion.' Howell was laughing now. 'Cuz if you had, you'd know that a little scraggy lad like you's nothing like a lion.' He lunged forward, opening his mouth and roaring so that Rook jumped and leaned away from him. 'See what I mean. You're scared of your own shadow.'

'No, I'm not. I'm not scared of anything.' Rook's voice sounded less certain than his words.

'I bet you're not brave enough to rob the mail.'

'I bet I am.' Rook answered without hesitation.

'What? A kid like you? You've not got it in you.'

'I'm not a kid. My Ma says I'm four and twenty – nearly. And I'm not scared of robbing no-one.'

'Prove it.' Howell leaned back in his chair and drained his

beer. 'I bet there'll be quite a bit of money inside the letters in those mailbags. I'd split it with you.' He paused, scarcely bothering to hide the greed in his eyes. 'I'll make it worth your while.'

Rook bit his lip. 'But it's against the law to steal.'

Howell's face expression was sneering. 'Backing out already? I said you were a ninny. Frightened your ma will tan your skinny arse?'

The younger man's face flushed red. 'Ma's never hit me. She wouldn't.'

Howell shook his head and went to the bar to replenish his tankard. He returned and shoved a glass of small beer towards Rook. 'Here you go, lad. See if that'll help you find a bit of backbone.'

∼

THEY PERFORMED the robbery the following day. Rook couldn't believe how easy it was. They met the mail boy on the road, a slip of a lad, riding on horseback and ready to hand over the sack of mail without argument as soon as Howell demanded it. They hadn't even needed a weapon. Just as well as they didn't have one. Their only concession to the crime was wearing handkerchiefs over the lower halves of their faces. They watched the postboy ride away and then, dragging the sacks of mail between them, headed for a barn where they set about tearing open the seals on the letters, discarded them and stacked the paltry contents in a small pile. Apart from a half sovereign, there was nothing of much value, just love tokens, pressed flowers, the odd sixpence.

'Is that all?' Howell scowled. 'I was sure there'd be more. No money orders. Damn it.'

That evening they were in the Red Lion, enjoying another ale together, with the meagre proceeds of their crime.

Rook leaned towards Howell, stretching out his hand for the half sovereign Howell was holding. 'Just a little look. I've never seen one before. I'll give it back.' Howell handed the coin over then snatched it back and pocketed it.

'Shall we do it again tomorrow?' Rook's voice was eager. 'We might get more money next time.'

'Idiot! Doesn't your tiny little brain work at all? That post boy will have reported it. They'll have the constables out watching.' Howell rolled his eyes.

Rook's lip trembled. 'Will they catch us?'

'Course they won't. Not if you keep your trap shut. We'll lie low for a bit and then maybe in a few months we can try again. Or find something better to rob. I'll hang onto the coin until then. We can split it when we've more loot to make it worthwhile.'

Rook sipped at his mug of ale, then grinned. 'So I am brave aren't I, Eddie? Brave as a lion.'

Howell shrugged. 'If you say so, lad. Not that there was much call for bravery. All we had to do was ask that mail boy to hand the mail bag over. *He* certainly wasn't brave as a lion.'

Savouring their beers, they were oblivious to the presence of a woman sitting in a corner behind Howell, a fishwife who was a habitué of the Red Lion. She had listened to every word and now slipped out of the pub to find the parish constable.

~

THERE WAS VERY LITTLE MOONLIGHT, so it took the old woman some time, bent double against the wind and rain, to stumble her way to Goldstone Bottom. As she moved along the road she saw two dark shapes outlined against the blackness of the night. Every time she made this pilgrimage it took her by surprise when she saw them swinging there, as if she had hoped it had all been a dream.

The metal cage creaked in the wind as it blew through and banged what was left of the two bodies against the bars. She knelt down in front of the cage and prayed. Eventually she looked up and whispered, 'I heard you calling me tonight, Jamie. I always hear you. I knew you was crying for me.'

The old woman shuffled forward on her knees and stretched her hand inside the cage and felt around. The metal was ice-cold and she found nothing. She ran a hand underneath the bottom, feeling blindly, her fingers scrabbling in the dirt.

Yes. She placed what she had found into the large pocket of her apron. Storms and rain and frost were all good – the bones fell off faster. Patience had been needed over the months and years as the flesh and clothing rotted away and the bones fell like over-ripe fruit from the tree that was her son's body, for her to harvest from the ground below.

She shivered and was conscious of the frailty of her own bones. She wouldn't be much longer for this world. Soon she would join him. But first she needed to gather every bone as it fell from his skeleton. They would join the others in the chest at the foot of her bed until she had them all.

It was hard to feel charity for Edward Howell. The older man had led her son astray, taken advantage of his slow wits to encourage him to join him in the crime. But the two men swung side by side on the caged gibbet so it was impossible to distinguish her Jamie's bones from Howell's, leaving her no choice but to collect his too. She swallowed her resentment. If only she had known what was going on. It had probably been a minor diversion for Howell. He was a reckless character. Bitter bile rose in her throat as she thought of the judge putting the black cap on his head and intoning their sentences. Two lives for a few coins and a pile of lost letters.

When she had visited him in the gaol they only let her see him for a few moments. Not long enough to say goodbye properly and tell him how much joy he had brought into her life. She had only had time to cling to him weeping, stroking his hair, breathing in the smell of him. The warden had pulled her off him and dragged her from his cell, slamming the door behind her, shutting out her boy's cries. Did he understand he was going to be hanged? Was he afraid? Why wouldn't they let her offer him some comfort, help him find a way to bear it, to be brave.

She felt the weight of her grisly haul as it dragged on her apron and she made her way back to the cottage. Soon she would have all her boy's bones and then she would make another journey, again under cover of darkness. This time her fingers would scrabble in the earth inside the churchyard as she buried the bones in hallowed ground, where no one else would know he lay.

# NO CRIME ON THIS ISLAND

## THE INDIAN OCEAN, 1980S

*J*t's time to leave the beach. We're sunburned and tired after an afternoon in the sun, swimming and snorkelling. I look at my watch. 'We're going to be late for dinner if we don't get a move on.' I change into my jeans and pull a tee-shirt on over my bikini top.

'It's only just gone four – what's the panic?' says Cathy. She's still soaking up the late afternoon sun and I can see her skin is reddening.

'We're on the far side of the island, it gets dark really early and we don't know the roads,' I say.

'There are so few roads we can't possibly get lost. Don't get your knickers in a twist!' She pulls a face.

We gather up our gear and get into the car. Cathy is still wearing her swimsuit with a pair of shorts on top. As usual I'm driving. When we arrived on the island two weeks ago Cathy declined my suggestion to add her to the insurance on our "unofficial" hire car, arranged with a friend of our hosts. 'I'm not driving that rust bucket,' she'd said.

I'm hot, sandy and tired and can't wait to get in the shower, wash the sand away and slather on the after-sun. I'm relieved that tonight there's no diplomatic reception to attend. These parties were a novelty at first – free flowing booze, lots of people and an excuse to get dressed up, but after a few nights of small talk with local dignitaries the allure has palled and we're both looking forward to a quiet dinner with our hosts. We have just one more full day after today and then it's the flight back home.

After driving twenty minutes we reach a fork in the road. One route circumnavigates this side of the island and the other goes straight over the top. We know the longer coastal route as we came that way this morning, but surely the road through the national park will be quicker and we might even catch the sunset.

We argue pointlessly about which way to go. Neither of us is sure and the argument is more about why neither of us is prepared to make a decision. Petty resentments surface. Tired of waiting, the engine of the car revving alarmingly, and with no stomach for bickering, I make my mind up and drive ahead on the upward track into the national park. Over the top it is. Cathy throws me a look and I know she wanted to go the other way. Too late now.

The road is steep and the old Honda is groaning. Despite the advancing hour the air is still hot.

'I wish we'd got a proper hire car at the airport instead of this old banger,' I say. 'I don't think it was actually any cheaper and it's seriously underpowered.'

'Stop moaning.' Cathy is in a bad mood.

'You don't have to drive it.'

Before she can reply the engine starts to make sputtering noises like an old man with a bad chest.

'Shit! There's smoke coming from the bonnet.' Cathy's voice is shrill. 'Stop the car!'

I pull over to the side of the road and realise the temperature gauge is in the red zone. 'Engine's overheated.'

We look at each other, neither of us wanting to acknowledge that the sun is now very low in the sky and we have no water.

''I told you not to take this road,' she says.

'You bloody didn't. You just kept telling me to make my mind up as I'm the driver.'

She scowls and is about to answer when she jerks the door open, leaps out of the car and runs in front waving her arms in the air. A police jeep is descending the steep hill towards us. I sigh with relief but the jeep accelerates away, passing us and disappearing into the trees below.

'Bastards!' Cathy slumps back into her seat. 'They bloody saw us. They must have done.'

'What are we going to do now? We can't just sit here all night waiting for the engine to cool down. We have to find some water. It's that bloody radiator the woman warned us to keep topped up.'

'Shit. Shit. Shit.'

'We should have got a proper car hire. This rusting pile of junk is only fit for the scrapheap.' I look around us. No houses. No cars. No nothing. Just trees and the mountain road rising above us.

'I'll flag someone down. Someone's bound to have a bottle of water.' Cathy is always good in a crisis. She gets out of the car and stands in front at the ready. No sign of a car.

Over the next ten minutes three cars pass us going down the hill. Two drive past without stopping and the third has no water.

I look at the dial and see the red line has moved back into the black. Not much, but it is just over the border. Must be the cool of the advancing evening. There is a distinct chill in the air now.

A large white four-wheel-drive Toyota pulls up beside us. Four men. They're young. Well dressed. The driver winds down the window and asks what we're doing. He smiles. Apologises. They have no water. He leans back into the car and consults with his companions in their local language then turns back to us. One of the men has got out and is coming over to our car. The driver says in perfect English, 'It will be dark in ten to fifteen minutes, we will drive behind you in case you break down. We can get water up at the top of the mountain in the national park. Drive really slowly and you'll be fine. We'll be right behind you.' He smiles. He has a handsome face. Dark hair, glasses. I smile back. Relieved.

Meanwhile the short guy who's got down from their car is opening the rear door of ours and is making himself comfortable in the back seat, sitting in the middle, leaning forward into the front between Cathy and me. 'I come with you. I keep an eye on the temperature dial. Take it slowly.' He has a cheeky grin.

I look at Cathy and she shrugs. I let out the clutch and the car splutters forward. We're doing about ten miles an hour. He asks us where we're staying and why we're visiting the island. We tell him we are holidaying with friends who are in the British diplomatic service. He prattles on about the island, recommending we try a beach on the opposite side, asking if we have been to a nightclub that he likes.

It's a relief to know we have help and that one way or another we will soon have water in our radiator and will be on our way. The man is pleasant enough. Younger than us. Probably mid-twenties. His English is pretty good, but not as fluent as the driver's. I concentrate on the road and on steering my steady and stately funereal progress up the steep road to the summit.

A house appears on our right and I say, 'Why don't we stop here. They can give us water.'

'No need,' he says. 'There's a water tap at the summit. We're nearly there.'

A few minutes later we are at the top of the hill. There is a sign showing a map of the national park and displaying the regulations. The other car pulls up behind us.

We all get out.

I open the bonnet while the driver takes our empty plastic water bottle and goes to where the tap must be. I lean into the engine housing, feeling the heat burning my face. One of the young men fetches a cloth to unscrew the radiator cap. I can hear Cathy talking to the one who had accompanied us in our car. I can't see them as they are behind the car and the bonnet obscures my view.

The driver hands me the full bottle of water, and taking the cloth form his friend, he bends to unscrew the radiator cap. I pour the water into the radiator and then hear Cathy screaming. Desperate screaming. Her voice is strident. Hysterical. Terrified. Begging.

'Let me go! Take your hands off me.' I hear the ripping sound of fabric tearing and then sobbing and her voice pleading with him to stop. I rush towards them but the driver steps in front of me and throws the radiator cap in my face. I feel the heat and hardness of it as it hits me on the temple. I turn to him in shock. 'What the hell are you doing? Stop your friend. He's hurting her.'

Cathy is now in full view, her swimsuit torn at the shoulder where he has ripped through the strap, revealing one naked breast. I turn to the driver who is blocking my way, one of his friends beside him. The smiles have gone. They won't let me get past them to help her. The fourth man is out of sight. The two move towards me.

I look up the road ahead to where a glorious sunset is washing the hills. Time has slowed down. There is silence. Cathy has stopped sobbing and shouting. I know we are both going to die. The irony of being murdered on holiday in a place of such magnificent natural beauty strikes me. I take in the scenery, certain that it is my last view on earth. I look up at the dying blaze of sun and experience the terrible knowledge that there is no way to wind the clock back. No more choices. No way to take the other road. No way to undo what has been done. Too late to have thought of packing spare water in the boot. Too late to have gone for the more expensive car hire instead of the friend-of-a-friend's. The bitter irony of this being a paradise island that they claim to be entirely free of crime. All this happens in what seems like many minutes but can only be a couple of seconds. A terrible sadness descends on me that it should come to this, that my life should end this way, in violence in a lonely spot on the other side of the planet from home.

A shout. A different voice. The missing fourth man. I realise now he has been at the back of our car. The boot is open. He is calling the names of his friends. He has our cameras round his neck and Cathy's rucksack over his shoulder. The driver and his friend move away from me, heading back towards their big white car. Cathy is screaming again. Her attacker won't let go. The driver guns the engine and at last the man pushes Cathy away, knocking her to the ground. He runs over to their car, jumps in and they spin the car around and drive away from us back down the mountainside the way we had come.

I turn to Cathy. She pulls her torn swimsuit up and gets in the car. She screams at me. 'Drive! Drive!'

'I need to find the radiator cap. One of them threw it at me and it landed in the grass.'

'Drive the fucking car!'

By now it's pitch dark and I'm torn between a desire to put my foot down and the certainty that if I do the radiator will run dry, helped by the fact that its contents are probably slapping over the road in the absence of the cap.

We head on across the dark deserted national park trying

to put as much distance between us and the men as possible – fearful that they might change direction and come back to pursue us. There is no traffic. Not a living soul. The sky is black, pierced by a million stars. No moon. Just acres of national park – a dark lonely mountain.

Somehow we make it back to civilisation, arriving three hours later than our hosts are expecting us. We shower and change and by the time we come downstairs a police officer – the island's chief honcho judging by the amount of militaristic gold braiding draped over his epaulettes – is waiting to interview us. We have no illusions. He looks pissed off and doesn't give a damn about us – he's only here because our host is the most senior British diplomat on the island.

He wants us to come to the police headquarters to make a statement. Cathy refuses. She's still in shock. I go, accompanied by our host. I get the feeling we're just going through the motions and the island's "finest" are unlikely to find our attackers – or even to bother trying. The police chief is angry because I failed to record the car registration number. No allowance for the fact that I didn't think we were going to emerge alive from the experience.

He asks what we lost in the robbery. I tell him we have both lost our cameras and wallets with cash inside. Cathy has lost credit cards too. Mine were back at the house as I didn't see the point of bringing them to the beach. The worst is that Cathy has lost the letter her father wrote before he died last year along with her favourite photograph of him. The police chief looks bored.

I tell him that we tried to flag down a police car which saw us but didn't stop even though it was obvious we had broken down. He shrugs.

At last I'm permitted to return home, feeling as though I'm the guilty party.

Next morning two policemen arrive at the house spinning the gravel under their wheels as their vehicle screams to a halt in the driveway. They escort Cathy and me back to the scene of the crime. It looks such a peaceful, harmless place in the daylight. We find a piece of the strap of Cathy's swimsuit lying on the grass verge but no sign of the radiator cap or any of our stolen belongings. The policemen drive us back to their headquarters. We pass a huge grey building surrounded by barbed wire in the middle of nowhere. A few days ago our hosts pointed it out and told us it was the island's prison. 'They have no crime here,' our host had said, his voice sarcastic. 'Yet this prison is bursting at the seams and there are plans to extend it.' He told us you don't have to be found guilty here to end up in prison – being a suspect is enough and the jail is full of men languishing in captivity for up to two years awaiting their hearings.

At the station the angry police chief appears again. This time he asks Cathy for the car registration number. She is cold. 'Funnily enough I didn't stop to memorise the numbers while I was fighting off the man who was trying to rape me. Maybe I should have asked him for a pencil and paper.'

The chief walks out in disgust, pausing at the doorway to say, 'Without the registration number we are unlikely to trace them.'

I call out. 'What about the car? A big white Toyota 4-wheel drive. New. Expensive. There can't be that many here?'

He curls his lip again and doesn't dignify me with a reply. His expression tells us it is our fault for having the temerity to be women. And to be driving a car. The absence of the radiator cap doesn't help our case. And the piece of swimsuit could have come from anywhere. One of the officers reminds us that there is no crime on this island. 'We are law-abiding people here.'

They think we are liars. Or that we have brought the attack upon ourselves. We both know that the police are thinking we got what was coming to us. I am glad they don't know Cathy was wearing very short shorts.

We are shown file after file full of photographs of known criminals. Huge lever-arch files. I look at Cathy and know we are thinking the same thing. All these criminals on an island that has no crime.

It's a pointless exercise. The men in the photos are unkempt, dirty, poor. Our attackers were well-dressed and looked like they had come from a country club not from a ghetto. More than likely our attackers are respectable sons of men like the police chief. We look at each other and know that this is a piece of window dressing to appease our host and not for us or with any intent to catch the criminals.

The next day we are getting ready to leave when the woman who has rented us the car arrives to collect it. I can hear her talking in the drawing room to Sue, our friend, who is telling her what happened to us. Then she leaves.

I had expected the woman, Sue's friend, would have been embarrassed about how her clapped-out, unroadworthy car had almost caused our deaths. But no. Sue says she asked for more money to recover the replacement of the missing radiator cap.

At the airport we sit in silence, surrounded by happy home-bound tourists, our own two week holiday blighted. Any happy memories are now overshadowed by what happened on that hilltop. I watch the clock, tense, counting down the minutes until our flight is called, desperate to be safely on board the plane and heading for home. I vow I will never return to this crime-free paradise island.

# THE OLD PALS' REUNION

## 1921

*T*he Ex-Servicemen's Reunion was the highlight of the year for Bill. Men only of course, it took place in a hotel in the city centre. It was a rare excuse to leave behind the responsibilities of married life and fatherhood and let his hair down in the company of other men he'd served with on the eastern front.

The attendees came from all walks of life. If it hadn't been for their shared experiences in Belgium and later in Prussia, they would have had little in common. But now even though they met only once a year, they picked up the dropped stitches of their comradeship as quickly and easily as his wife did with her knitting.

In the normal course of events Bill rarely drank. There just wasn't the money for it. He had to make a choice between beer and tobacco, and the cigs always won. They'd be the next to go of course, with Fanny in the family way and the town council cutting wages yet again. It was the second time this year they'd had a pay-cut. What was it Mr Micawber had said? "Annual income twenty pounds, annual expenditure nineteen pounds nineteen and six, result happiness. Annual income twenty pounds, annual expenditure twenty pounds and sixpence, result misery". They were definitely drifting dangerously close to misery.

But tonight was his night. Fanny hadn't complained about him going. Not that she ever had or ever would. He'd found a gem in her. She didn't know the half of what he'd been through in the war but she understood it was more than any mortal man should have to bear.

'All set?' she asked, coming into the back kitchen, her hands in the arch of her back, her pregnant belly extended before her like a ship in full sail.

'You sure you don't mind me going?'

'Of course I don't.'

'You mean you won't miss me?'

'Of course I will.' She flicked at him with a tea towel.

'In that case – yes. I'm all set. Fingers crossed it will go off all right. If it doesn't, it's down to me this year.'

'If it doesn't, it'll be down to them. No one could have worked harder than you have to make sure it goes like clockwork. It'll be the best Old Pals "do" they've ever been to.' She stretched a hand out and stroked his cheek.

He leaned in to her and kissed her tenderly. 'What would I do without you, Fanny?' He grabbed his raincoat and hat off the hook on the back of the kitchen door and put them on.

'Aren't you forgetting something, Bill?' Fanny moved over to the table and picked up a cardboard tray full of crepe paper poppies. She took one out and opening his raincoat, threaded it through the buttonhole of his jacket. 'Can't have you not looking the part tonight.' The poppy was huge and red, like the buttonhole a circus clown would wear to squirt water from. She stood on tip toes and kissed him.

Bill grinned at her. 'The lads are going to love these. You've done us proud.'

'I'm proud of *you*,' she said, smiling. 'Enjoy yourself – but not too much!'

Balancing the tray of poppies across one arm, Bill left the house and headed down the hill to pick up the train into the city.

The evening was a uproarious success. While the core purpose was to celebrate their miraculous survival of the "war to end all wars', and to honour the memory of those comrades who had not managed to share their good fortune, the opportunity to let their hair down and share a few bevies in what were undeniably hard times, was too good to be taken lightly. The men sat at a long table and enjoyed a meal of fresh grapefruit, roast beef with boiled potatoes and a pudding of apple pie and custard, all washed down with plenty of beer. Bill glowed in the compliments of his fellow diners at the quality of the food and was glad he'd chosen the grapefruit instead of the Brown Windsor Soup, the hotel had tried to palm off on them when he was making the advance arrangements. Nothing like the clean sharp taste of citrus – a rare treat.

The poppy buttonholes had been the perfect finishing touch and he was grateful to Fanny for suggesting the idea and then spending so much time making them for him. He looked around the table and felt a surge of satisfaction, seeing his comrades all sporting them proudly.

The hand-drawn programme of events had gone down well too – souvenirs for the lads to take away and treasure. It had been a stroke of genius on his part, though he said it himself, to get Ronnie O'Hara, who was a dab hand with the old pen and pencil to illustrate the programme with caricatures of the principle speakers. Fanny would have a laugh when he showed her. Old Ronnie had caught him brilliantly, megaphone in one hand, hair standing on end, with the caption "Bill, The Labour Agitator" – they all knew how hard he'd been campaigning against the council pay cuts.

Then there were the speeches, One or two were long and rambling and full of sentimentality, but the best, short and funny, focused on shared anecdotes and memories and the human desire to find humour in even the grimmest of situations. No one who hadn't served in the war could ever hope to understand the bond they shared. The knowledge that each of them would have gladly laid his life down to save another. When war was as bad as they had witnessed, their own individual lives ceased to matter, sublimated into a desire to do the best for the collective group.

Bill got to his feet to make the toast to absent friends, a final moment of respect to the men who didn't make it. The two-minute silence in the room was electrifying. All those present, even the waiters, stood with heads bowed.

*Cockadoodledo!* – the strident cry of a full grown rooster cut through the solemn moment. It came from a cardboard box, placed by Fred Watkins on the top of the piano. Any tendency towards the lachrymose was dispelled by the incongruity of the cockerel crowing as it pushed its head through the top of the box, escaping the dark of its captivity.

'What the...?' For once Bill was lost for words. All the heads turned to look at the rooster as it crowed raucously on the piano top.

Fred Watkins was shamefaced. 'Sorry, lads. Never trust children and animals! The wee bird has got a bit ahead of itself. No sense of theatrical timing.'

'A bloody chicken? What they hell are we doing with a bloody chicken?' Bill didn't know whether to laugh or cry. His dilemma was resolved when, after a stunned silence, the men began to crow with laughter and then all broke into a rowdy chorus of cock-a-doodle-dos, the real thing adding a descant over the top.

'Sorry, lads. I reckoned our Bill's singing needed a little bit of help,' said Fred, interrupting the cacophony. 'The wee birdie has come along to support him when he gives us his fine rendition of *"I'm homesick for the hills"*. The entire company began to stamp their feet and bang their fists on the table, chanting "I'm homesick for the hills" until Bill took his place beside Fred at the piano and began to sing the song. The sadness of the lyrics and the tune were rendered into high comedy as his singing of the melancholic air was accompanied by the crowing of the rooster. Any hurt pride on Bill's part was wiped out by the knowledge that the gathering was going with such a swing that it would be talked about by the attendees for a long time.

When finally the event drew to a close, hurried along by the Maitre D' pointedly tapping his watch and signalling to Bill, the verdict that this was the best reunion ever was unanimously declared. After a chorus of *"For he's a jolly good fellow"* in honour of Bill's organisation skills and the success of the night, the party broke up.

Bill staggered through the city streets to the station, accompanied by Fred Watkins and a couple of the other fellows. The rooster, which Bill had to acknowledge was a fine young bird, if a little on the scrawny side, had refused to go back in its box and was now held in the arms of Watkins.

By now Bill was pretty tight. It was so rare he had an unfettered opportunity to imbibe alcohol for an entire evening and he saw no possible objection to Watkins pressing the bird into his arms when his train arrived on the platform.

'You take him, Billy Boy. You have the shortest journey home and he did such a grand job at accompanying your singing. It's a great chance for you to perform as a double act again. How about at the parish concert?'

Bill could find little to argue with that. Besides, it was a cold night, his raincoat was thin and the bird was a as warm against his body as a hot water bottle. He staggered onto the train and took his seat, waving goodbye though the window to Fred, and cradling the bird against him. It was a few minutes before he noticed the woman opposite staring at him and realised it was a woman he knew vaguely from church. She was nudging the woman next to her and they were whispering and giggling. Bill decided to behave as if travelling at 11.30 at night with a sleeping rooster in his arms was the most natural thing in the world. He raised his hat in greeting, then stared out of the window until he reached his stop, bidding the women goodnight before stepping off the train.

Next morning, he had no recollection of the walk home from the station and surmised it must have been more of a drunken stagger. He slept in late, it being a Saturday, until the scent of bacon drifted up the stairs and he dragged himself out of bed, cursed his hangover and went down for breakfast.

Fanny didn't look at him when he walked into the room. She silently placed his eggs and bacon in front of him and poured him a cup of tea.

Bill tucked into his breakfast. There was nothing to beat a bit of bacon when you had a raging hangover. Fanny was a holy treasure and a mind reader into the bargain.

'Was it a good night?' she said eventually.

'It was a cracker, though I say so myself. The best reunion we've had yet. Everyone said so. They want me to organise next year's as well.'

Fanny scraped a bit of butter across her toast. 'Your little friend is in the yard.'

Bill scratched his head. 'What friend?'

'I don't know his name but he appears to have spent the night in the sitting room.'

Bill cranked his head round. 'He did?' He wanted to ask who it was, but didn't want to indicate to Fanny that he had been too drunk to remember which of his pals had come back and bunked down on the settee for the night. 'You think he wants some breakfast?'

'It looked like he'd already got through half a packet of porridge, so I don't think he needs anything else right now.'

'Porridge?'

'Well Quaker Oats. Uncooked.' Fanny popped the last bit of toast in her mouth. 'He's out in the back yard now.'

Bill grunted. 'The back yard? Is he having a smoke?' He pulled his chair back. 'I'll tell him he can have it in here. It's too chilly to be outside.'

'I doubt he's smoking. I've never seen a chicken that knows how to smoke a cigarette.'

Bill dropped his knife and fork. 'Holy hell! I forgot about the blasted chicken!'

'I'll be getting porridge oats out of the sitting room carpet for months I reckon, not to mention the unspeakable stains out of the settee. Whatever made you think the sitting room was a good place to keep a chicken?' She got up and took her plate over to the sink. 'What on earth were you doing with it in the first place? And why in heaven's name did you decide to bring it home with you?'

Bill swigged his cup of tea and reached for the pot to refill it. The memory of the previous night was now in vivid colour. What the deuce had persuaded him to bring the stupid rooster home with him?

'Oh, Fanny, I'm so sorry. What have I done? Can you ever forgive me?'

Fanny poured herself another tea from the pot and sat down. She leaned towards him and put her hand over his.

'Oh, yes, my love. I can certainly forgive you. As soon as you get yourself and your new friend along to the butcher's and find someone to dispatch the poor creature. He's far too scrawny and probably tough to make a roast Sunday dinner tomorrow but I'm looking forward to a delicious chicken broth tonight.'

# CHAPTER 1 OF THE CHALKY SEA

EASTBOURNE, ENGLAND, JULY 1940

*T*he sea was pearl grey and sparkled like the scales on a fish. Gwen stood at the window staring at it, as she often did. A few miles away in France, armies of German soldiers were probably staring back across the Channel wondering what lay ahead of them. Since the terrible events of Dunkirk the previous month, Gwen had been oscillating between fear and hopelessness. The German invasion was coming, and defeat was an inevitability. Belgium, Holland and France had fallen, crushed under the onward thrust of German panzers, so what chance did Britain have?

She sensed Roger as he came up behind her. He placed his hands on her hips, then she felt the touch of his lips on the back of her neck. She stiffened and took a half step forward.

'Time to go, old thing,' he said.

Gwen turned to face him, her mouth forming an artificial smile to reflect her husband's real one. 'All set.' She dangled the car keys in front of him.

Roger reached for her hands, gripping them tightly as she resisted. 'Look, darling, I want you to promise you'll go across to Somerset to stay with Mother. I don't want you staying here. Things are going to get nasty.'

Meeting his eyes she smiled. 'I've told you. The moment the house is empty they'll requisition it. I don't want a lot of airmen in hobnail boots scratching the surface off my parquet floors. Half the road has already been taken over by the RAF.'

Roger moved his hands up to her shoulders. 'Once the war gets going properly – which will be any time now – we'll have more than scratched floors to worry about. Hitler won't bother to requisition the place. He'll just rain bombs down on it.'

'On Eastbourne? Don't be silly, Roger. He's not going to bother with a little seaside town. He'll want to flatten big cities, docks, factories. I can't imagine him sitting down with the Luftwaffe and targeting the pier and the Winter Garden.'

Roger let his hands fall. 'I wish you were right.'

'Of course I'm right. Don't you worry.'

'Gwennie, you know as well as I do that the invasion will happen here or near here. You can't possibly stay. The whole south coast is pitted with tank traps and covered in barbed wire.'

'Well that will keep the Germans out,' she said brightly. 'I promise you, at the first sign of an invasion, I'll drop everything and leave. Meanwhile I've things to do. There's the WVS. I can't let them down. So many have already left the town. Someone has to keep the flag flying – at least until we know how things lie. I want to move things into the cellar and the attic, out of harm's way in case they do requisition the house. As soon as I've done that I can go to Somerset.' She spoke the words and hoped he wouldn't know she was lying.

Roger sighed but said nothing more.

They passed the ten-minute drive to the station in

silence, each conscious that this morning marked an indefinite period apart. It might be months, years even. He might never return but neither wanted to acknowledge the fact. After his escape from Dunkirk Gwen thought they may have used up all their good fortune.

The station concourse was crowded. There were young men setting off to join their regiments for the first time, women and children belatedly evacuating the coast where plans were advanced to counter the German invasion. Not so long ago the traffic had been in the other direction, when the town had opened its doors to give a rather grudging welcome to thousands of evacuees from London. They had all returned home or gone elsewhere as Eastbourne transformed into a frontline town, ready to stand hard against the German invasion that was expected imminently. Now the station, which used to be adorned with colourful hanging baskets, was lined with sandbags. Propaganda posters were plastered over walls that once advertised the attractions of pleasure boats and the programme of entertainment at the Royal Hippodrome and the Devonshire Park Theatre.

A month ago the first sign of German aggression had been witnessed by the town when a merchant ship, laden with food supplies, was bombed off Beachy Head. Gwen had watched the burning vessel from the balcony of her bedroom. It seemed unreal. Like watching a news reel at the cinema. The war was no longer something happening on the other side of the Channel or flickering in black and white across the big screen.

A small group of uniformed officers were waiting apart from the crowd at the far end of the platform. Roger nodded at them then turned to say goodbye to his wife. He bent his face to kiss her, but she turned her head slightly so his lips met the hard edge of her jawbone rather than her mouth. She gave him another tight smile and said, 'Buck up, darling.

Don't let's get all soppy. The war will be over before too long, then things will get back to normal.'

Roger glanced towards the colleagues who were watching curiously. He swallowed and ran his hand through his hair. 'Look, Gwen, I'm not supposed to say this, but you need to understand. This war isn't going to end quickly and it's going to get very ugly. I can't even tell you where I'm going – I don't know yet myself, or when I'm going to see you again if I make it out the other end. I might be sent somewhere where I can't get word to you, but, Gwen, wherever I am, I will try and get in touch. If you don't hear, it won't be because I didn't try. I love you and I'll miss you every second I'm away.' He pulled her towards him, crushing her against his chest.

Gwen breathed in the familiar smell of him, felt the rough scratch of his uniform jacket against her cheek. She felt small and fragile when he held her, trapped, captive, like a caged bird. She stood rigid, willing him to release her and for the moments to pass until she could leave him to his colleagues and take herself outside the noisy station and away from him. Away from the possibility that he might see her mask slipping. That he might notice that her lip was trembling, that she was fighting back tears.

At last Roger drew back. He held her shoulders and looked down into her eyes. 'Gwennie, old thing. I love you so much but I know I've been a disappointment to you as a husband. I'm sorry.'

Panic rose in her when she saw his eyes were damp. She reached up and planted a quick kiss, square on his mouth. 'You are a silly sentimental thing. You know I hate that kind of talk. And it's not true anyway.' She tried to make herself say the words he wanted to hear, but they wouldn't come. Instead, she said, 'I'll miss you too, but the time will pass quickly. Now it looks like those chaps over there are waiting for you to join them, so I'll head off.' She gave him another tight, hard-lipped smile and turned and half ran out of the station.

There was a Local Defence Volunteer standing guard over her car when she emerged onto Terminus Road. 'You can't park a vehicle here, Madam, it's an exclusion zone.' He swaggered up to her, shifting his weight so that the rifle casually slung over his shoulder would be evident.

Gwen threw her handbag and gas mask carelessly onto the passenger seat, settled herself into the driver's, and fired up the engine. The LDV man stepped in front of the car, blocking her path. She engaged the reverse gear, then realised her retreat was blocked by a heap of sandbags. The man banged loudly on the roof of the car.

'What do you want?' she said. 'I'm moving the damned car.' As she looked him in the face for the first time she thought he looked familiar.

He drew himself up to his full height then bent down and leaned through the open window. 'I'm only trying to keep everybody safe, Madam. I was about to tell you that you can park across the road there.'

She remembered where she'd seen him before. He was a pump attendant at the petrol station. Always ready with a cheery greeting and an offer to wash her windscreen when she stopped by. Ashamed, Gwen gushed excessive apologies then put her foot down. Damn the bloody war. After a few hundred yards she realised she was crying. She pulled over and dabbed at her face with a handkerchief. For God's sake, Gwen, pull yourself together, woman.

Jerking her handbag open, she took out her compact and powdered her nose. After applying lipstick, she inspected herself in the mirror. No evidence of the tears. She snapped the compact shut, put her hands back on the steering wheel and took a few deep breaths.

Roger's departure had hit her harder than expected. She would be rattling around that big house on her own, no one to eat with, no one to share a sherry. And no one to share her bed. Not that Roger was unreasonable in that respect. When children had not resulted after several years of marriage, Gwen was grateful that he had not brought the subject up. It was as if he had sensed that it was a topic she wanted to avoid. Too painful to be confronted. Once it was tacitly agreed there wasn't going to be a baby Roger didn't expect her to let him make love to her so much. Maybe once a month, unless he'd had a few drinks – that always made him amorous. Otherwise he left her alone, to her relief. No, she couldn't complain. She was grateful. Roger was a decent man. Yet that morning he'd said he thought he'd been a disappointment to her.

Gwen couldn't imagine what he meant by that. Lack of children aside, their marriage was probably no different from the other couples in their circle They rarely argued. They muddled along fine. She certainly wasn't disappointed in him. Leaning back in the seat she sighed. Disappointed in life though. In marriage as an institution. In her lot.

Endless dull days when nothing happened. Her world contained by the house. Her purpose to plan meals, brief the cook, oversee the housekeeping. Her recreation the odd round of golf, tennis in summer, the weekly bridge game. She had never got round to telling Roger she didn't even like playing bridge. What was the point? At least it occupied an evening every week.

She envied Roger. He'd had his legal work with the Foreign Office to occupy his days. He'd travelled a lot with the work, often abroad, and, since the advent of war, he'd been involved in something top secret that meant he spent most of his time in London and closeted away in meetings at destinations to which she was not privy. If she had been frustrated with her lack of purpose before the war, now she felt more so. Roger wanted her to run away and wall herself up in a cottage in Somerset with his mother. There was nothing wrong with Maud. Gwen liked her, but she didn't want to spend the duration of the war with her, filling her days with knitting squares for refugees and growing vegetables.

The town was deserted. On a whim she parked the car and decided to walk the mile and a half up the steep incline back to her home in the district of Meads. She needed to work off her nervous energy. After a few minutes she took off her jacket. The day was already getting hot despite the still early hour. She wiped her brow. You're out of condition, woman, she told herself. That's what comes of a life of idleness.

~

THE FOLLOWING SUNDAY soon after eleven, Gwen was sitting on the terrace drinking tea. In front of her the sea was the colour of pale peppermint and milky with chalk washed from the cliffs.

She sipped the weak tea and grimaced. It was like dishwater. She would never get used to rationing. She would never get used to the war. At first she had thought, guiltily, that it might at last bring some meaning into her life, give her something to think about, something to distract her from the emptiness inside. She'd joined the WVS and supervised the dispersal of evacuees around the town, mended soldiers' socks for the war effort, and made endless pots of tea. But it was window-dressing. Inside she believed the war was already lost and the disaster that was Dunkirk had reinforced that. Gwen wasn't going to let herself be afraid. She had a plan. As soon as the invasion began she was going to down the contents of a bottle of codeine she'd set aside for the purpose and fall into a grateful sleep. Death was not to be feared. She had no idea what life under a Nazi occupation would hold and no wish to find out. If she were honest, she was using the invasion as an excuse.

In the distance, the faint sound of anti-aircraft fire grew louder. The low buzzing thrum of planes – ours or theirs? Was the invasion starting now? As the questions were forming in her head they were interrupted by the boom-boom-boom of a series of rapid explosions.

She spilled her tea on her dress as she jumped to her feet. Behind her the windows were rattling in their frames. The house faced south so she couldn't see the town, but already a plume of smoke was moving out over the sea. The war had come to Eastbourne. There had been no warning.

# CHAPTER 2 OF THE CHALKY SEA

ONTARIO, CANADA, JULY 1940

*T*he sun was sliding low in the sky, a rosy glow spreading over the distant horizon behind acres of ripe wheat. Jim Armstrong rubbed the back of his neck where the sun had caught it. He'd forgotten his hat again. He reached down and grabbed a handful of ears of wheat, rubbing them together in his hand then blowing off the chaff to leave the plump grains. It was ready. The combine would be arriving tomorrow and it would take them a week to harvest the crop if they put their backs into it.

Jim loved this part of the day. Work over. Supper soon to be on the table. A chance to slake his thirst with a cool beer after a long, hot day, and now a leisurely stroll back to the house with the dog by his side, alone with his thoughts. Over the past months since war was declared, the news reports and the recruitment posters all over town had made him ashamed to be still here on the farm. So many of the men he'd grown up with and gone to school with had left for Europe as soon as Prime Minister Mackenzie King announced that Canada was at war.

Europe was thousands of miles away and their war wasn't

his, but he couldn't help feeling he ought to be playing his part. After all, Canada was part of the British empire. His father had been involved in the last war and had a boxful of medals to prove it. There was a legacy to live up to. The old man had done his bit and now it should be the turn of Jim and his brother Walt to do theirs. But every time he'd tried to talk to his father, Donald Armstrong changed the subject. He hated any mention of his time in the trenches and always brushed off attempts by his sons to draw him on his wartime experiences. As for Jim's mother, whenever he or Walt broached the idea of joining up, she burst into tears.

Jim's dog, Swee'Pea, was sleeping under a tree at the far edge of the field. The dog was getting old and these days seemed to sleep more than he was awake. Jim had rescued him years ago as a puppy, when he found him floating in a sack in the creek, abandoned, presumably the runt of the litter. He'd christened him after Popeye's foundling baby in the cartoons. Swee'Pea wouldn't be much longer for this world. Jim couldn't imagine life without him.

He made his way slowly back towards the distant buildings, Swee'Pea trailing behind him. No sign of Walt, but that wasn't unusual. Probably fishing in the creek along the edge of the farm. Any opportunity to duck work and Walt took it. It annoyed their father but Jim always indulged his younger brother.

There was plenty of time to take a bath before supper. While meals were usually informal in the Armstrong household, he was going to make a special effort tonight as Alice was coming over to join them. He wanted to talk to her again about his dilemma over whether or not to join up – although he guessed what her opinion would be. She'd prick his bubble, remind him that it was someone else's war, half way across the world, and that they had plans to marry next summer. He smiled as he pictured her narrowing her eyes and frowning at him in mock disapproval – she was always good at bringing him down to earth. He couldn't wait for next year to come, when at last he could have her to himself, when at last she would be his completely.

Spruced up, shaved and wearing a clean shirt, Jim sat down at the kitchen table. His father was already seated.

'Wheat's ready. I ordered the combine for tomorrow,' Jim said.

'Didn't you say Alice was coming to supper tonight?' his mother asked, as she carried a pot from the stove. 'I've made butter pies. Not like her to be late.'

Jim shrugged. 'I expect she got held up at the library. She'll be here soon.' He nodded towards another empty chair. 'Where's Walt?'

'Went to check on the cow,' said Donald. 'Maybe she's started. Not due for a few days but you never know. Why don't you go and see if he needs a hand?'

Helga Armstrong sighed. 'Dinner will be spoiled if you have to sort that cow out.'

'Cows don't care about mealtimes. When a calf's coming it's got to come.' Jim pushed his chair back and got up from the table.

The porch door opened and Walt came into the kitchen. He pulled out his chair and sat down. 'I've a right appetite tonight, Ma,' he said. 'What's for supper?'

'Nothing for you until you've scrubbed yourself up. We've company tonight. Alice is joining us.'

Walt sighed, got up and left the room.

His mother called out behind him, 'And a clean shirt mightn't hurt if you've been messing around those cows.'

A few minutes later the porch door rattled and Alice came into the kitchen. 'I'm so sorry I'm late,' she said, her face flushed and her voice breathless. 'I got here as fast as I could but that old bike was hard work tonight. Seems the whole town brought their books back today.' She gave Jim a quick kiss on the cheek and sat down.

Jim waited until everyone was tucking into the peameal pork and baked beans, then said, 'I saw Petey Howardson this afternoon when I went into town to book the combine. He's had letters from his boys.'

Walt looked up. 'And?'

'They haven't seen any action yet. Seem to be stuck at training camp. Nine months now. You don't go to war to spend all your time on exercises.' Jim shook his head.

'Better not to go to war at all,' their father barked.

'Thank God, is what I say,' said Helga. 'I feel for those Howardsons. Three boys and all of them joined up and overseas. I pray their poor mother will get them all back safely when it's over.'

'The war to end all wars. What a joke that was. Barely twenty years later and they're expecting more men to throw their lives away.' Donald shovelled a spoonful of beans into his mouth.

Alice tried to steer the conversation onto safer ground. 'How are the Howardsons coping without the boys? Must be hard work for Petey.'

'Mrs Howardson and the two girls are working hard and there are half a dozen kids who come by at the weekends and after school to lend a hand. The school has organised it that the older kids get off an hour early. Petey says they're coping fine.'

Donald raised his eyes from his dinner. 'I know where this is heading, son, and that's an end to it. Easy enough for Petey to get by with women and children – he's only growing vegetables and keeping cows. And two of those boys of his were worse than useless, specially that no-good Tip. It's a different matter here. We can't get by without you two.'

Helga wiped her hands on her apron and stood at the end

of the table behind her husband. 'What happens over in Europe is nothing to do with us, son. You're not expected to go and fight. You're needed here. The Prime Minister made it clear that fighting this war was voluntary. If Canadians were really needed they would be conscripted. Those Howardson boys were always work shy. Anything to get off the farm.'

Jim looked across the table at his brother, waiting for him to say something, but Walt stayed silent.

'Every time I go into town I feel people looking at me. I know what they're thinking. That I'm chicken. Afraid to defend my country.' Jim turned towards Alice but she was looking down at her barely touched plate.

'Defend your country?' Donald slammed his fist onto the table. 'No one's attacking your country. If Hitler invades Canada then you can join up. Until then you're staying here. No son of mine is going to go through what I went through. Not while I've breath in my body.'

Jim looked over at Walt who was frowning and scraping at the surface of the tablecloth, where one of the threads in the cloth was fatter than the others. He ran his fingernail over it repeatedly, as though trying to scratch it down to match the size of the other threads. Why wasn't he jumping in to support Jim?

'It's not about defending our borders – Mr Mackenzie King said it was about defending all that makes life worth living.' As Jim said the words he felt embarrassed. They sounded hollow coming from him whereas over the radio when the Prime Minister declared the country to be at war they had sounded noble, inspiring, compelling.

Eventually Walt looked up. 'If Jim wants to go, then maybe he should. I can stay and help Pa with the farm.'

Jim's mouth fell open. It was not what they'd talked about. How many times had they walked on the banks of the creek discussing joining up together? Walt had, if anything, been the prime mover. Right from last September, when Mackenzie King declared the country was following Britain into war against Germany, he had wanted them both to defy their father and volunteer.

Donald leaned back in his chair. 'This is the last time I want to hear about this. You're a grown man, Jim. I can't stop you, but if you do go, then don't bother coming back here afterwards. If you think risking your life for strangers is more important than supporting your own family, I've raised you wrong.'

Helga put a restraining hand on her husband's shoulder. 'That's enough of that kind of talk, Don.' She turned to Jim. 'Don't you be paying attention to what other people say. Your responsibilities are here. And talking of running off to war when you've a wedding to plan – shame on you, Jim Armstrong. Staying right here growing wheat and corn to feed the troops and send to those poor folk in England is what will make the biggest contribution to this war.' She smoothed down her apron. 'And I don't want you over there killing Germans. Remember your own grandmother was German. I was brought up German. Hitler may be a bad man, but all those German soldiers are young men like you and Walt. I don't want any son of mine killing anyone. That's the end of it. Now, who wants one of my butter pies? I made them specially for you, Alice.'

'You're spoiling me again, Mrs Armstrong,' said Alice.

'If I can't spoil my future daughter-in-law, who can I spoil?'

Alice tucked an escaping strand of hair behind her ear and blushed. Jim looked at her and wondered, as he often did, how he'd managed to persuade the best-looking girl in the district to marry him. Her hair was pale blonde, shot through with the colour of ripe corn when the sunlight was on it. He had to fight the urge to run his hands through it whenever he saw her. When she smiled she lit up the room, her eyes as blue as cornflowers and her lips full, revealing a slight gap between her front teeth. His heart pounded as he looked at her. It almost killed him not touching her whenever she was close: it was like a child being left alone with a piece of candy and being told he mustn't eat it. When he looked at her, the thought of joining up was less appealing. How he could he bear to be parted from her?

'Stop that.' His mother was addressing his brother. 'You'll tear a hole in my best tablecloth.' She slapped him lightly on the arm.

Walt got up from the table. 'I'm going to check on that cow again.'

'You'll go nowhere. We have a guest. Have you no manners?' Helga reached out to grab her son's arm, but he was too quick for her and left the room, the door slamming behind him.

'What's got into him?' Helga shook her head.

'I'll go after him,' said Jim half rising from the table.

'Leave him be,' their father growled.

The tension in the room was palpable. After a few minutes Alice looked at Jim, then got up and said it was time she was going.

'I'll walk you home.' Jim was on his feet.

Alice laid a hand on his arm. 'No, Jim, I came on my bicycle. I'll be fine. Thank you so much, Mrs Armstrong. It was delicious, especially those butter pies.' She waved at Donald and went out of the door, Jim following.

On the porch he pulled her towards him. 'Shall we walk down by the creek for a while? We haven't had a minute alone.' He bent to kiss her.

She eased herself away from him before their lips touched. 'I have a summer cold coming on and I don't want to give it to you,' she said. 'I don't feel too great so I think I'll head on home. You go inside. It's getting chilly.' Before Jim could respond, she had stepped off the porch and was running towards the fence where her bicycle was leaning. He watched as she mounted the bike and pedalled away down the track.

Jim had no wish to sit in the kitchen with his parents and open the argument again. He wished them goodnight and told them he was going upstairs to read a book. In the room he had shared with Walt since they were small children, he lay on the bed and stared at the ceiling, thinking of Alice.

She had been in Walt's class at school. Alice was a little kid with pigtails. He hadn't noticed her until one day when he saw her in the school yard, surrounded by boys who were trying to persuade her to kiss them for five cents a go, that he really saw her. Alice was up against the wall, like a trapped animal. When he approached, her eyes fixed on him, uncertain whether he was about to add to her troubles or be her rescuer. He looked at the gang of boys and saw Walt was one of her persecutors. Jim had gripped his brother by the collar and shoved him away. 'Leave her alone, you're a bunch of bullies,' he'd shouted and was rewarded with a smile from Alice that melted his indifference. She was thirteen and he was fifteen and from that point on she was devoted to him and he would have done anything for her. They started going steady the year Jim left school and had been together ever since, to Walt's initial disgust and eventual silent resentment.

Jim tried to read his book but tonight he was immune to the call of Jack London. Putting the book aside he got up and went in search of Walt. Maybe that cow was calving.

Swee'Pea followed him as Jim headed into the barn. He blinked as his eyes adjusted to the dark and shivered in the cool interior. There was no sign of Walt. The heavily pregnant cow gave a soft low as he approached then went back to munching hay. He ran his hands along her flank. Not ready yet. Maybe not until tomorrow. He was about to go outside and head back to the farmhouse when he heard a soft moaning. He looked about him. Apart from the cow the barn was empty. Another moan, louder this time and the sound of rustling straw. He looked up. It was coming from the hayloft.

Jim's heart began to thump in his chest with a sudden unaccountable fear. For some reason he didn't want to find out what was up there but felt compelled. It wouldn't be the first time he'd found hobos sleeping in the hayloft. A flicker of pain touched his right temple. He put his foot on the ladder and began to climb up.

Standing at the top of the steps he didn't see them at first. It was almost entirely dark up there but the loose roof panel that Donald had been nagging him and Walt to fix, allowed a narrow stream of light to penetrate the gloom at the rear of the loft. Walt, his overalls at half mast, was on top of a girl whose legs were wrapped around his back.

Walt had shown no apparent interest in girls. In fact Jim had begun to wonder if he might be inclined the other way and now here he was, doing the dirty with some loose woman. The sly dog. None of that lengthy courtship, waiting and holding back that he and Alice had undergone – were still undergoing. He'd too much respect for Alice to ever push her to go all the way before they were married, much as it nearly killed him, he wanted her so much. No such discretion for little brother – he'd gone right out there and rolled some girl in the hay. You had to hand it to him. Walt didn't believe in doing things by halves.

Jim was about to retreat discreetly, a smile on his face. He'd get some mileage out of what he'd seen – enough ammunition to tease Walt all winter – when the girl cried out. 'Oh God, Walt, what are you doing to me? I don't think I can take any more!'

At the top of the ladder Jim froze, his hands gripping the wooden struts so tightly his fingers were white.

Then her voice again. 'I didn't mean it! Don't stop! If you do I'll kill you.' Another groan.

The pain in his head grew, carving a path through his skull, blinding him. He swayed and clutched the ladder and the barn began to spin around him. Let this be a dream. Let me wake up. It's not true. How could it be true? Not Alice. Not Walt. They couldn't. They wouldn't.

Then they were looking at him, their eyes reflecting their horror back at him. Their shame. Guilt. They looked at each other and in that moment Jim knew his whole life was a lost cause. Seeing the look they exchanged was worse than witnessing what their bodies had done. It was a look of complicity, of shared understanding, of love.

He didn't wait while they scrambled to adjust their clothes. He slid down the wooden ladder, barely touching the rungs and began to run. As the twilight descended the sound of Swee'Pea's plaintive barking grew quieter as he ran until his lungs were bursting.

# ACKNOWLEDGMENTS

My first thanks go to my readers, some of whom have read everything I have written and constantly urge me to get the next book out. Unfortunately I can't churn them out as fast as many would like – I have to craft the books through numerous iterations before they are ready to be released to the world. I'm grateful to you all for your loyalty, encouragement and patience.

Thanks to my critique partners, Margaret Kaine, Jill Rutherford, Maureen Stenning (aka Merryn Alllingham) and jay Dixon. Your frank and constructive fortnightly feedback has helped me to hone these stories – and you always know when less is more.

Finally to my extended family – I have borrowed and distorted our history in two of these stories – A Fine Pair of Shoes and The Proposal. In the latter I had to reduce the cast for the sake of the story and have conflated two events for the same reason. Both stories are thus fiction – albeit with their origins in fact. I have also stolen snippets from my grandfather's correspondence and embroidered them for

The Glass of Milk and The Old Pal's Reunion. He died when my Dad was only thirteen so I never knew got the chance to know him but his letters have given me an insight into his life and his sense of humour.

# ABOUT THE AUTHOR

Clare Flynn is the author of four works of historical fiction with her fifth novel to be published in summer 2017.

A former Marketing Director and strategy consultant she was born in Liverpool and has lived in London, Newcastle, Paris, Milan, Brussels and Sydney and is now enjoying living on the Sussex coast where she can see the sea from her windows.

When not writing she loves to travel (often for research purposes) and enjoys painting in oils and watercolours as well as making patchwork quilts.

*Contact Clare*

www.clareflynn.co.uk
clare@clareflynn.co.uk

ALSO BY CLARE FLYNN

A Greater World

Kurinji Flowers

Letters from a Patchwork Quilt

The Green Ribbons

The Chalky Sea

To get advance warning of Clare's future publications, special offers and insider information please sign up to Clare's Readers' Club via her website at www.clareflynn.co.uk. You won't get spam – just occasional news and offers and you can unsubscribe any time. Sign up now and **receive A Greater World absolutely free**.

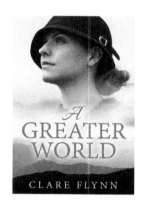

Lightning Source UK Ltd.
Milton Keynes UK
UKOW05f0327300617
304364UK00002B/68/P